BILLY THE KID

FRANK CARDEN

Produced by Flat Sole Studio,
a division of Skywater Publishing Company,
398 Goodrich Avenue, St. Paul, MN 55102
www.flatsolestudio.com

Library of Congress Cataloging-in-Publication Data
    Names: Carden, Frank F. (Frank Frazer), 1932- author.
    Title: Billy Bonney (aka The Kid) / Frank Carden.
    Description: Minneapolis : Flat Sole Studio, [2016]
    Identifiers: LCCN 2015044844 (print) | LCCN 2015048400
(ebook) | ISBN 9781938237188 (softocover) | ISBN 9781938237287
(ebook)
    Subjects: LCSH: Women outlaws--Fiction. | Billy, the Kid--
Fiction. | Outlaws--Fiction. | GSAFD: Biographical fiction. | Western
stories.
    Classification: LCC PS3603.A734 B55 2016 (print) | LCC
PS3603.A734 (ebook) | DDC 813/.6--dc23
LC record available at http://lccn.loc.gov/2015044844

Acknowledgment: I am deeply indebtied to my editor Blake Hoena
who had faith in my writing and published my first novel. He is more
than an editor; he is a friend.

Cover Photo: Cyndi Carden Myers

The fine editing by Susan Bagby and Susan Gomex was greatly
appreciated. Thank you both.

BILLY BONNEY AKA

THE KID

Enjoy the read.

Frank Carlen
Jan 11, 2018

FLAT SOLE STUDIO
an imprint of Skywater Publishing
http://flatsolestudio.com

This book is dedicated to Barbara J. Carden, my wife

Forward

In 2004, I found the first diary buried in a 1890s trash dump, while digging for old bottles west of Mesilla and east of the Rio Grande. The book of faded handwriting was in an ancient Wells Fargo wood and metal money box. It was written by a cowboy who rode with Billy early in The Kid's life.

The diary led me to a memoir, not much more than a writing tablet full of notes, also written by an individual close to William Bonney. My assumption is that the writer was a member of the McSween family. I decided not to reveal the writer's name for a number of reasons, all personal. This tablet was buried just outside the boundary of the old Maxwell ranch, near Fort Sumner, and it too was in a Wells Fargo money box. Inside was a tintype photograph of William Bonney, believed taken by a relative of Mrs. Susan McSween. This is the only known authentic photo of The Kid.

The diaries or memoirs, written mostly about Bonney, were by individuals whose relationships with The Kid are well documented in historical books. After carefully studying these personally recorded events and deeds of the participants of the Lincoln County War, I decided it was past time to write a true life story of William Bonney. In order to protect the privacy of the two writers' living descendants, it was occasionally necessary to change names, but never facts. Otherwise, in writing this story, I followed the diaries meticulously.

1

1875 May, Silver City, New Mexico Territory

Hearing a slight noise in the old barn, Wilma, a sixteen year old, stopped pitching hay to her horse and stood still. She smelled the man, whiskey and stale sweat, before she turned to face him standing behind her, close. Herbert was a deputy sheriff who lived with Sarah Brown, the owner of the house where Wilma roomed.

"Herb, what do you want?"

"You little pimp, I seen you bring cowboys in to see Sarah."

"Get away, you're all liquored up."

"It's time you started screwing for your own money." He grabbed her hair, jerking her backwards with one hand, his other grabbing at her Levis.

She struggled to get loose, but he was strong and six inches taller. When she stumbled back against the wall, he stepped forward, caught his foot in the trough and fell face down, only to roll over quickly and sit up. She grabbed a pitchfork and, using it like a bat, slammed its handle against his head splitting his ear.

Running to the front of the barn, she grabbed her pistol from the saddle bag.

He came toward her.

She stood still, the gun's barrel pointing downward, hanging easily.

"You point that pistol at me, I'll break your neck." But he stopped.

She didn't move, not toward him, not away.

"You skinny bitch, you don't know how to shoot."

"Try me."

He took a step, his hand jerking at his holstered pistol.

In one smooth motion her gun swung upward, her thumb cocking the hammer. The pistol, angling upward slightly, roared with a bright orange flash in the gloom. The forty-one-caliber bullet caught him just below his nose, right above the lip. It slammed through his teeth, tumbled sideways, slashed through his brain and jammed against his skull. His head jerked backward, his foot halted in midair, and he collapsed. She stood over him, pistol ready, but a bloody face and unblinking staring eyes told her there was no need to waste another bullet.

In less than fifteen minutes, she was back from her room, wearing stuff her brother had left—a dark wool shirt, leather vest, and a black beat-up hat. After saddling up, she rode slowly out of town because, even in Silver City, killing a lawman was big trouble although he had assaulted her. They would be after her for certain.

Wilma rode south-southwest toward Lordsburg, along the narrow wagon tracks. The thing was, she was the only girl around who wore trousers and a shirt, making her easy to spot. Spending a lifetime in jail would be hell for her. So, something needed to be changed. But what? As the lights of Silver began to fade behind her, she stroked gently with her spurs, causing the horse to increase his pace slightly. A notion suddenly struck her. She looked like a boy, with her wiry build, the smooth way she rode, her body contoured to the saddle. Enough men had told her that. Maybe that was it. Cut her hair short and pass as a boy.

Wilma's hand stroked her smooth chin. Even that wasn't a problem. Her brother was twenty-two and never shaved. She could get by as a boy, so why not give it a try? It was a disguise that would make it hard for someone to figure out who she really was. With her hair cut short, and acting like a man, no one would recognize her when she was fifty miles from Silver. She would head across the border into Arizona Territory and get a job as a cowboy on some ranch.

What she needed was a man's name.

From Wilma to William was not that far. What about a last name? Her mother had said something about a man back in New York, suggesting he was her real father, a Bonney. So get rid of Antrim and go with William Bonney. Okay, except that sounded kind of stiff, so make it Billy Bonney. All young cowboys were called kid, so they could call her Billy or kid.

Anyway what she wanted in life was to be free to ride, shoot and play cards like a man. But on Saturday night she enjoyed going to the dances and being treated like a woman. For now she would settle for the first three. Billy spurred the horse to a smooth lope, the Little Burro Mountains small black humps against the darkening western sky.

The Kid was on his way.

Earlier that evening, around sundown, Wilma had ridden her horse into the dilapidated barn, after practicing all afternoon with her .41 caliber Colt at an abandoned ranch house. From a tree in the yard she had grabbed a handful of green hedge apples, placing them on the wooden rail of a fence. At twenty paces she drew her Colt and, in the same motion, leveled the gun, thumbed back the hammer and shot. The end apple exploded. She practiced drawing a dozen times before firing again, blowing-up the second round green apple. Firing a gun was natural for her.

Joe, her brother, was the only one who knew how good she was with a pistol and, even though he had practiced with her and was also good, she could outshoot him five to one. He was the one who first got her interested in shooting. When she was ten, she had fired his

.38 pistol. The minute the gun bucked in her hand, with the muzzle blast pounding her ears, she was hooked. The noise certainly had not frightened her. The fact was, the power of what she held in her hand was exciting beyond anything she had ever done before. That passion remained with her each and every time she pulled the trigger.

Joe had left a week earlier for California. He hoped to get a job with the Central Pacific Railroad that was building a branch called the Southern Pacific to the Arizona Territory. She missed him.

Slender with small bones but wiry, she weighed just over a hundred-ten pounds and stood five foot six. Her small hands, with long slim fingers, were only as wide as her wrists. She had long brown wavy hair, slightly protruding teeth, and a flat chest. She was not especially attractive, yet the boys around town liked her, and she liked them.

Keeping the horse moving along wagon tracks now barely visible in the darkness, the pistol pulled forward, and resting on Billy's thigh, produced a sense of power. It always had. The thing was to get through Lordsburg without any trouble. Once past that small town, no one would recognize Billy as the person she had been.

2

In '72, the army moved Camp Grant from the San Pedro River to the base of Mt. Graham in the Arizona Territory. This placed the camp directly in the path of the rogue Apaches from the San Carlos Reservation, traveling south to raid down into Mexico. The army was to stop this. But we'd heard that the camp commander, a Major, was from back east and was not pleased with being assigned to that out-of-way place. He never led a patrol out looking for the warring Apaches, although he'd send out some dragoons under the command of a lieutenant.

The new Camp Grant consisted of eight adobe buildings in an L shape that partially enclosed a dusty parade ground with two cannons. The stable was on the east end of the L. The San Simone River was ten miles farther east.

Me and my friend Jesse Evans was in the vicinity of the new Camp Grant six years later in early Spring of '77 to buy some stolen horses from a man we knew as John Mackie. The horse I rode in on threw a shoe and we took it to Frank Cahill, the camp blacksmith. That day while we were waiting on Mackie and my horse, me and Jesse met Billy Bonney for the first time. To the west of the camp was Bonito, a small settlement of four adobe buildings. One was the Atkins's Cantina where Billy dealt cards.

That was the day Billy killed his first man that we knew of. Lloyd

Spring 1877

Billy and John Mackie herded six horses into a small corral built beside an arroyo south of Mt. Graham in Arizona Territory. It was a little after sunrise when they dismounted and closed the opening with two long cedar posts. Both rolled cigarettes and stood smoking, looking at the horses.

"I'm through," Billy said. "I've been rustling horses for two years, and that's enough. The ranchers are getting wise."

"Think you can make enough dealing cards?"

"Yeah, if not at Camp Grant, then someplace else." Billy shoved a worn boot onto the bottom rung of the enclosure. John had been a good partner, teaching Billy all about how to steal horses locally and then sell them to someone outside the Territory. In taking horses, Mackie always said take the well broken ones, the horses in the corrals. They were easier to handle, and would stay in a herd if not pushed too hard.

Since leaving Silver two years ago, Billy had been taught a lot and not just about horses. There had been two real shootouts, with a man getting killed each time. What Billy had learned watching the gunplay was that the man who drew first, who shot first accurately without hesitating, was the man who stayed alive.

"How we going to split the take? I got two guys coming from New Mexico to take the horses back there to sell."

"John, I'm out of it, you take whatever you get."

"Okay. That's the way you want it. You really don't give a damn about money, do you? Still, I ain't even seen you waste your money on liquor and whores."

Billy didn't comment. John was right about money, because it meant nothing just as long as there was enough to get by on. Billy was missing the dances they used to have in Silver and the boys, but that was something not to think about. The decision had been made. The past was the past for now. Some things changed and some things didn't. Billy's weight had increased by ten pounds, height by an inch, but she still had a flat chest and narrow shoulders with wider hips. Billy took a second long drag on the cigarette as usual, pitched it onto the gravel, and ground it out with a boot heel. Smoking was not all that enjoyable, except all the men around did it.

"Long as you got enough money to buy shells for that forty-one to shoot cactus pods when we're out riding, you're happy."

"That's about it." Billy mounted, swung the horse around and rode slowly down the rocky trail.

Late that evening Billy, with a cup of coffee in front of him, sat in the one room adobe cantina on the dirt road that wound through the saguaro cactus. Camp Grant and its cleared parade ground was a quarter mile away. Billy was dealing five-card stud to three soldiers drinking beer. They were playing for small stakes. At the bar, the husky camp blacksmith, Frank "Windy" Cahill, stood watching, throwing down a shot of whiskey and quickly refilling the glass from a bottle in front of him.

"I don't trust no kid dealing cards while he's drinking coffee," Frank said.

The four at the table ignored him.

"He cheats," Frank said, "especially when he gets the other players drunk."

Billy, both hands lying motionless on the table, looked over at the big blacksmith.

"I don't know why Major Johnson don't run him out of town. He's always taking you soldiers for your money."

When Billy started to ease out of his chair, one of the soldiers said, "Hell, don't mind him, he's drunk."

Frank emptied his glass, dropped a gold piece on the bar and turned to walk out.

"See you around," Billy said, hands still motionless on the table.

"You ever walk into my place, you ain't going to walk out," Frank spun to face the card players.

Billy just smiled, recalling the earlier poker game he'd played with the blacksmith, how the man tried to bluff and buy pots when he didn't have the cards, and Billy had called him every time, taking over a hundred dollars in gold pieces from him.

"Okay, Bonney. Have it your way for now. One day soon though I'll see you around." He walked toward the door.

"Anytime."

Several days later, early afternoon, two out-of-town cowboys rode in on one horse, tied him to the hitching rail. They now stood at the bar drinking whiskey. Billy sat at a table, watching, saying nothing but rippling the cards occasionally. Both of the cowboys wore dirty hats, one gray and one black.

"You the dealer?" the older, taller cowboy asked.

Billy nodded.

"Draw poker?" the younger one asked.

"Whatever strikes your fancy."

"Horse threw a shoe," the tall one said when they sat down at the table. "Getting a new one hammered on over at the blacksmith's."

Billy shuffled, dealing each man five cards. The young cowboy was attractive and had a nice smile with white teeth and, though he did less talking, he was clearly the boss, picking the game, the chair he wanted. They played six or seven hands, staying about even, before the cowboys ordered another round.

Billy dealt.

"You sure got nimble fingers," the tall cowboy said.

"Meaning?" Billy looked at him then placed the card deck on the table.

For a moment no one spoke.

Billy's hands lay on the table, motionless.

"Hell, meaning nothing. Just you're a good dealer is all."

Billy nodded with his eyes on the tall cowboy.

"Let's go check on our horse," the good-looking one said.

The two got up and Billy followed them out the door. As they walked along, Billy slowly drew his pistol, careful to point it away from the cowboys as he spun the cylinder.

"Why the hell you checking that gun, just going to see the blacksmith?" the young cowboy asked.

Billy shrugged.

At the corral two troopers sat on the top rung watching Cahill shake Joe, a small Arivaipa Apache kid, one taken for cheap labor.

"Go get his horse," Cahill ordered Joe, slapping him across the back of his head. "When I tell you to do something, do it pronto."

Billy leaned back against the corral, one boot heel hooked on the bottom rung, elbows resting on the fourth one up.

When the Apache kid finally managed to get the bit in the horse's mouth and the bridal buckled, he brought out the horse. The tall cowboy lifted the horse's left rear hoof and checked the new shoe.

"Good enough?" Cahill asked, hands on hips, staring at the man.

"Yeah."

The blacksmith grabbed the small boy again, "Don't you know what pronto means?" He raised his arm.

"Cahill," Billy said, still leaning on the corral, "don't hit the kid again."

He turned to Billy, letting the boy go.

"You're a sonofabitch," Billy said. "And you called me a cheat."

The two cowboys backed away.

Cahill glanced at a sawed-off shotgun, a Greener leaning against a post.

"Go for it," Billy said.

Cahill grabbed the gun, swinging it toward Billy, thumbing back both hammers.

The forty-one slug caught the blacksmith beside his nose just below his left eye, knocking his head backward. His fingers jerked the triggers firing both barrels, shattering a corral rail two feet from Billy. Cahill crumpled down to the hard-packed earth.

Billy turned away from the man on the ground and looked at the two troopers. "You two stay around, the sheriff's going to be here shortly. He'll want to talk to all of us."

Later back at the cantina, the three of them stood at the bar, the two cowboys taking shots of Double Anchor whiskey and Billy drinking his coffee.

"Lloyd." The tall cowboy stuck out his hand, "And this is Jesse Evans."

"Billy Bonney."

"That was something," Lloyd said. "You didn't even move until the blacksmith had that shotgun swinging. That took nerve, ain't that right, Jess?"

"I suppose."

"Billy, you sure got guts, and you're fast, fast as anyone I've ever seen."

"Except me," Jesse said, looking at Billy, eye-to-eye.

"Billy's awful fast," Lloyd said.

"Maybe one day we'll find out," Jesse said.

"Let me tell you something," Billy said, still eye-to-eye. "Don't ever try me."

Abruptly Jesse turned and motioned for another round.

"With the sheriff calling it self-defense," Lloyd said, "you got off okay."

"Yeah, maybe. Depends on the Major, he runs things here."

"If there's a problem, you can always go with us," Lloyd said.

"Yeah?"

"Mesilla, over in New Mexico Territory."

In the sheriff's office, the Major stood in front of the sheriff who was sitting at his desk in the small adobe building.

"Even your two troopers said it was self-defense," the man with the star pinned to his shirt pocket said.

"Sheriff, Bonney instigated it. Besides, Cahill was the only blacksmith in a hundred miles."

"It was self defense."

"You're here because I asked for a lawman. You do something about it or I will."

"You want me to arrest him?"

"For criminal and unjustifiable murder. My men will testify Billy provoked it."

"Arresting Bonney might not be so easy." The sheriff stood.

"Hell, he's just a kid."

"A kid, yeah, but damn good with a gun from what your men said. And I mean good." The sheriff walked over to the open door to look down the dirt street at the cantina.

"You want help arresting some kid, I'll send a few of my men with you."

"I'll handle it, there's not going to be a shootout." He faced the Major. "And if there is, I think your men will come out on the short end."

"You have till tomorrow." The man in the blue uniform walked out.

Around midnight Billy, Jesse and Lloyd sat at one of the two tables in the cantina playing poker. Most of the coins were in front of Billy. Two women sat at the other table, watching the game but saying little.

"I like the young one. Half-Mex, half-Indian?" Lloyd said.

"Hey, Rosie." Billy waved her over. For several minutes Billy and the girl talked back and forth in Spanish after she sat down at their table.

"You sure speak that Mexican lingo good," Lloyd said. "As good as a Mex."

Billy asked another question then placed some coins in her hand.

"She your girlfriend?" Lloyd asked. "Or you getting her just for the night?"

"Neither," Billy said. "It's a week till the soldiers' payday. Things have been slow. She's got a kid."

"So, she's available for tonight."

"She could use the business," Billy said.

"How much?"

"One peso, all night," Rosie said.

Lloyd pulled a coin from his pocket and gave it to her. She spun around and sat down in his lap, her arms around his neck. In a moment both got up and walked out to a small adobe room built onto the cantina.

"Well," Jesse said, "it's just you and me and the bartender. Not much fun playing two-handed poker." He flashed Billy his fine smile. "Any other women around? That other one there is too old for me."

Billy watched him for a moment. Two people playing poker wasn't much fun. Jesse was good-looking and had a cocky walk, swinging his narrow hips just enough.

"Indian woman or Mex, don't make any difference to me," Jesse said.

"It's a little late, all the Indian women are already bedded down." Billy placed the deck on the table and finished the coffee all the while looking at Jesse's brown eyes, almost black in the dim light from the kerosene lamp hanging from a ceiling beam.

"You'd think, here at an army post, there ought to be women hanging around."

"Payday, that's when they drift in." Billy scooted the chair several inches closer to Jesse.

When footsteps sounded outside, Billy turned toward the door his hand sliding quickly to his pistol.

The young Apache boy, Joe, ran in and looked at Billy. "Sheriff said tell you, he's going to arrest you. Tomorrow, one hour after sunup."

"Okay." Billy handed him a coin. "Now get out of here. And Joe, you tell the sheriff thanks."

"Well, Billy, you ought to just go with us," Jesse said.

"Might as well."

"Ain't no place to sleep around here. When I finish this drink, I'll get Lloyd and we'll head out. But we got to make a little detour first, see a man by the name Mackie."

Billy smiled, "Sounds okay to me."

3

Diary, page 5

Billy had dark blue eyes, always sparkling. He whistled softly when ambling along, even after he shot the blacksmith. A strange man, killing didn't bother him, nor did he seem to tense up when it looked like there was going to be gunplay. In talking to the blacksmith just before the shooting, his voice was soft and pleasant, almost like a woman's. Now Jesse and Billy got along good except something would come up, nothing important, and it put them eye-to-eye, each ready to outdraw and shoot the other. Then it would blow over and they were back to their friendly ways. Billy would look at Jesse as if he was the best buddy in the world while they talked about wild times, whores and gambling. But there was something about Billy— like killing was just something to be done such as taking a drink of water. I saw that part of him again when we run into a small group of Apaches. That's when I made up my mind. Ole Lloyd was getting away from these guys. I had seen some shooting, but with Billy there was just a feeling that bullets were always going to be whistling by. And I wasn't going to mess with him, a smiling man or not. He'd put a slug square between my eyes before my pistol ever cleared leather. I knew that for a fact. Lloyd

Jesse, Lloyd, and Billy picked up the six horses, five dollars apiece, from Mackie. Billy smiled at his horse-stealing buddy, but said nothing when Jesse paid him off with two gold coins. They headed southeast and swung west of the small town of Safford toward Apache Pass, following the San Sabine River with the water reflecting the dim light from the stars. South of Safford they passed a small ranch with four horses in a corral.

"We might as well take those too," Jesse said.

"That's John Clapton's place," Billy said.

"Yeah?"

"Take three of them, but not the black."

"How's that?' Jesse rode over close to Billy, stirrup-to-stirrup, facing him.

"The black is a fine racehorse. He's worth more than we can sell him for."

"That's Clapton's problem," Jesse said.

"The black's not going." Billy's hands were crossed on the saddle horn.

A dog barked from the ranch house less than a hundred yards away. Billy kept his eyes looking directly at Jesse, his horse motionless.

"Well, hell, okay if it means that much to you, we'll take the three." He swung his horse away from Billy.

Lloyd opened the gate without dismounting and kept the black in, while the others joined the six Billy and Jesse kept together. Quickly they disappeared in the tall saguaro plants and clumps of prickly pear cactus.

By noon they were to the north of Fort Bowie, close to Apache Pass where a small spring was located. They followed the old path of the Butterfield Stage along Siphon Arroyo. The deep tracks of the coaches' large wooden wheels remained visible between the rocks protruding from the sandy bottom. An early summer wind from the north had come up whistling, rattling the yucca pods and the mesquite branches. It was tough seeing ahead with all the dust in the air, and hard to breathe even with their scarves pulled up over the lower half of their faces. Coming around a tight bend, they ran into three Apaches leading two fully loaded packhorses. The Indians had good looking Mexican saddles on their horses and Winchesters resting on their wide cantles. They had been raiding down in Mexico. Everyone stopped.

"A shootout here this close is going to get everyone killed," Jesse yelled above the roar of the wind. "We'll just ease over among the rocks. Let them pass."

A gun blasted three times, sounding like one continuous roar. A forty-one slug caught the nearest Indian in the middle of his forehead, knocking him backward. The two Indians behind the packhorses crumpled with single bullet holes in the center of their chests, their rifles falling to the ground. None of the three had a chance to cock their Winchesters. The horses reared kicking up clouds of sand, their hoofs clattering on the rocks.

Billy holstered his pistol, rode ahead and grabbed the lead rope on the packhorses, calming them. Lloyd had slid from his horse and stood, pistol in hand, peering from behind a large rock. Jesse was still mounted, staring at Billy who pulled down his scarf and gave a big grin. For a minute, no one said anything.

"Those Indians, they weren't going to let us pass. It was just a matter who shot first," Billy said. "They wiped out a small wagon train last month."

"Jesus," said Lloyd, holstering his gun as he moved from behind the rock to look down at the first dead Indian.

"San Carlos Apaches," Billy said, "not Geronimo's warriors or we'd still be shooting. Anyway looks like we got us some more horses."

"Jesus," Lloyd said again, jerking his bandanna off and wiping sweat from his face.

The saddled Indian ponies had run off into the hills and were out of sight in the blowing dust. No one gave chase.

"Hides and ammunition," Jesse said, inspecting the packhorses Billy was holding. "I know a man in Lordsburg we can sell this stuff to."

Billy slipped off his horse and picked up the three Winchesters looking them over carefully, jerking down the levers, ejecting the shells from the chambers. He aimed the newest, chambered a shell, and fired at the fork of a mesquite tree on the hill, splitting it.

Jesse and Lloyd stared at him.

"This one is in really good shape, a Winchester 73. I'm keeping it. We'll sell the other two." Billy mounted and the three started pushing the horses ahead, leading the packhorses.

"We need to head a little northeast, hit the wagon trail on the other side of Fort Bowie, bypass it," Billy said.

At mid-morning, the three stopped on the wagon trail east of Lordsburg to give their horses a breather. The day before all the stolen horses and hides had been sold to the rancher south of the small town. They had stayed at the ranch overnight sleeping in the barn on bales of hay and talked about going to Mexico.

To the northeast Cook's Peak loomed against the blue sky, which was no longer hazy, the dust storm having blown itself out. At its base, but not visible, was Fort Cummings.

"I'm heading back to Mesilla," Lloyd said. "I'll cut a little north from here and hit the fort. You boys go on down to Chihuahua."

"We got the money to have a good time there," Jesse said. "Lots of tequila and plenty of whores."

Lloyd looked at him but said nothing else, their two horses neck-to-neck facing ahead.

"Hate to see you miss the fun," Jesse continued.

"Think I'll just head back."

"You might as well go with us," Jesse said.

"The hell with it," Billy said. "Lloyd, if you want to go with us, go. If you don't, don't. We ain't begging you."

"Well, I guess I ain't going," Lloyd said.

"Fine." Billy looked at Jesse. "Come on, we'll have us a baile. I'll guarantee. Just the two of us."

Jesse nodded.

Billy suddenly pulled his recently acquired Winchester from the new scabbard he'd bought, jacked in a shell, and fired ahead of Lloyd and Jesse at a running coyote crumpling him into a furry ball. The two men jerked around in their saddles to stare at Billy who grinned at them.

"We'll see you in Mesilla," Billy said as he shoved the rifle back into its boot. He kneed his horse and slowly rode away to the south.

4

Early Friday morning two week later Billy and Jesse rode into Chihuahua. They had stopped at small towns along the way, but mostly had been riding from sunup till several hours after sundown, covering three hundred miles of desert. Finding a stable, they sold their horses and bought two fresh ones. Across the street at a small café, they ate a big breakfast of steak, salsa, tortillas, and beans, with black coffee.

Farther down the same street, they rented a hotel room. Jesse poured water from a pitcher into a glass bowl and washed his face before he pulled off his boots and peeled off his shirt and Levis. With his long johns on he stretched out on a side of the one bed, pulling the blanket up over his shoulders.

Billy walked around the room several times, pushed a chair over next to the bed and sat down. It had been a long ride with both of them sleeping in their clothes, lying on their saddle blankets covered with jackets, heads resting on their saddles. She leaned back in the chair, looking across at Jesse who had already started snoring. Getting in bed with Jesse, it was going to feel strange actually in bed with a man, not like rolling in the hay with the young kid back in Silver. She stood and walked over to the dresser. Before stripping down to her baggy worn out long johns, she splashed water on her face from the basin and wiped it off with the small wet towel that Jesse had used. It smelled of his sweat.

The sunlight angled in from the window. For a moment she stood, looking down at the street below that had become busy with men on horses and a few women walking by.

Carefully sliding under the blanket, Billy got into the bed and lay facing the ceiling, feeling the heat from Jesse's body. She closed her eyes to shut out the light and lay there. She didn't feel sleepy. When he moved and the mattress sagged, she eased out of the bed and pulled the shade down.

In the dim room she stood beside the bed while Jesse continued to snore. Across the room on a chair were his clothes—a bright red shirt, faded but neat Levis, and scuffed but not run-down boots. She looked at her worn boots by the bed and her torn Levis on the back of the chair. The first thing she was going to do was buy some new clothes, also some more long johns and maybe a new coat or leather vest.

Jesse was now lying on his side, facing away, his rounded but slightly pointed hip sticking up against the blanket accentuating his narrow waist. His legs were stretched out straight and spread, his left foot on her side of the bed. She took a deep breath and considered having some hot water brought up to the tub in a back room to wash and soak in while he slept. Still watching Jesse's hips and legs, she sat down softly on the edge of the bed. The bath could wait. Carefully she slid under the blanket, keeping her foot away from his left leg, closing her eyes. Her body was tired and trying to relax. But sleep wouldn't come. She moved her foot slightly touching Jesse's. A warm flush crept from her thighs to her waist, continuing to move upward. Her small nipples hardened, sticking out against the soft cotton top of the long johns. It had been a long time since the boy in Silver. Stretching her leg out straight, she rubbed her calf softly against Jesse's heel, warm and smooth. She lay without moving, her leg resting against his foot. She considered getting out of bed, stripping, getting back under the cover, grabbing his hand, and placing it between her legs. Those thoughts made the yearning even more intense.

When Jesse moved slightly, she jerked her foot back and turned away from him, willing herself not to move. After his snoring started again, she climbed slowly out of bed, pushed the chair over to the window, rolled the shade up a foot, cracked the window slightly and looked down at the people but reluctantly glanced back at the bed.

Billy rolled a Bull Durham and sat there smoking. Damn it. When she was riding, firing a gun, or playing poker, thoughts tumbled through her mind as though she was a man. But when she got around an attractive man, she thought and felt like a woman, just like what she was. She couldn't have it both ways, not now anyway, although it was aggravating to have to pose as a man to do the things she wanted.

Her cigarette a stub, she pitched it out the window to the dirt street. The warm sun streaked under the shade, hitting her midsection. Finally, her head tilted forward as she began dozing off. Easing out of the chair, she walked softly back to the bed, slid under the quilt and lay quietly on the edge of the bed as far from his body as she could get. Her eyes closed and sleep came.

It was late afternoon as both walked across the street to eat again, the only two Anglos in the restaurant. Billy ordered large steaks, speaking in English. When the meals came with a big bowl of Mexican rolls, they ate without looking up or talking.

"I'm going over to that tienda, the mercantile," Billy said when the waitress was clearing the table, "and get me some more clothes before we hit the cantinas."

Jesse grinned. "Want to look good for the señoritas?"

"Yeah!"

"First thing for me is a big shot of tequila. Billy, how come you don't drink?"

"For one thing, I'm going to gamble. A drunk loses money."

"Well, the next thing for me is to find a good looking Mexican girl and spend some of my money. How about you?"

"Same here," Billy said, and stared out the window at the women walking by before turning to face the man across the table. "Yeah, that's something I need to do."

The two had been in the cantina all night, Billy gambling and losing at four-card Monte. Jesse had been drinking shots of tequila and had gone to bed several times with different women. By dawn, Jesse had a new woman.

"Cash me in." Billy pushed his small pile of chips over to the dealer, stood and stretched.

"Me and Josie are going over to her place," Jesse told Billy, empting his glass of tequila, while she buried her face in his neck, biting at his ear.

Billy nodded. "What about breakfast?"

Jesse grinned. "Later."

"You coming back to the hotel?"

"Sometime."

"See you then, whenever," Billy said as he watched his friend and Josie walk out the swinging doors of the cantina. Jesse looked good in his red shirt with the tight Levis hugging his slim hips and the well-worn Stetson cocked to the side. And he still managed to swagger even with Josie giggling and holding on.

Billy walked out and stood on the sidewalk, looking down at the new boots with the jeans tucked in. The new black leather vest felt good in the early morning coolness. The couple were a block down the street, their arms still around each other. Where her place didn't concern Billy but, wherever it was, Jesse was going to enjoy it. Which was fine, except… Well, that was that. If Jesse had gone back to the hotel with Billy, then what?

Billy slowly rolled a cigarette from a sack of Bull Durham, looking at the round white cylinder with its twisted, crinkled end, finally placing it between dry lips and striking a match across the tight blue denim. Inhaling deeply, Billy looked down the street one last time, watching Jesse and Josie, before turning to walk toward the hotel.

5

Jesse and Josie came into the cantina around midnight. Saturday night the place was full. Billy was hot with tall stacks of red and blue chips in front of him. He had switched to playing three-card Monte always betting on the spade being matched if one came up. Otherwise he passed. By three in the morning the bar was no longer packed. There were three Mexican gamblers sitting at Billy's table, with Gonzales the dealer. The bartender leaned on the counter, watching the action. Three women sat at another table while Jesse and his girl stood at the bar, drinking tequila.

After Billy raked in a large pile of chips, he stood and motioned to the girl called Lupe sitting at the other table. "Come on over here." He handed her a coin. "Let's go to the room outside for a quickie, keep my luck going. Jesse, you watch my chips."

The other gamblers glared at Billy and the stacks of chips but said nothing. He didn't know whether they understood English or not. The talking was and had been in Spanish, except for Billy, who had always made the bet and card choice in English, never speaking Spanish. He was not going to let the Mexicans know he understood what was being said, sometimes even asking the dealer to repeat something in English.

Lupe shoved the coin in a pocket and grabbed Billy's hand and both walked out a side door. Jesse sat down at the table while the dealer continued to deal, turning up three cards and, after the betting, one card at a time.

Twenty minutes later Billy, followed by Lupe who was not smiling, walked back in buckling his belt. The card playing halted, but the men at the table continued to talk to each other in Spanish. Billy stopped at the table and looked at his chips, arms folded, saying nothing but finally using both hands, bent over and aligned the stacks.

"Hey, Jess," Billy said when his friend stood. "Before I sit back down, I need to take a leak, grab some fresh air. Come with me."

"How was she?" Jesse asked when they stepped into the outhouse, a two-holer.

"Not bad, the usual, but Jess, here's the thing. I gave her ten pesos." Billy leaned against the wall, hands on hips, making no effort to unbutton.

"Ten pesos! For one piece of ass?"

"Yeah, for her to tell me which hotel Gonzales stays at. And I promised to come back and kill her if she told anyone about me asking. Or if she lied to me."

"What the fuck's going on?"

"The game's over, and Gonzales is not going to pay me for my chips. It's rigged,"

"That's what there're saying?"

"Yeah." Billy opened the door a crack. "And we can't do nothing about it here. They got us four to two. Don't make any fast moves, give them an excuse to pull on us."

"Yeah, yeah, okay. You want to jump him at his hotel."

"Before he gets there. Lupe told me about an alley, we can get ahead of him."

Billy walked back into the cantina and sat down at the table. His friend followed and stood at the bar with Josie away from the two girls at the table. Lupe sat stiffly at another table, alone.

"I'm through for the night," Jesse said. "Go sit at a table, Josie."

She looked at him, frowning, but turned and did as she had been told.

"Guess I'll cash in." Billy shoved his chips across the table.

Gonzales, ignoring the chips, raked his stacks of doubloons into a leather sack. "Got to pay you tomorrow, not enough money tonight." He grabbed all the chips. "But I'll count them." He placed the chips in long rows of stacks of five.

The other men pushed their chairs back from the table.

No longer leaning on the counter, the bartender stood-up straight. His hand found the handle of a drawer and slid it open.

Billy smiled. "You pay me about noon, tomorrow? That's when I get up."

"Si," Gonzales said.

The other three players kept their hands resting on their thighs.

"Here?" Billy said.

"Si," Gonzales repeated.

"Sounds okay to me." Billy slowly stood, hands on hips, away from his pistol.

Jesse started backing toward the door.

"See you around twelve," Billy said. He turned his back to the table and walked out.

Billy and Jesse unhitched their horses, mounted and rode slowly down the dirt street. At the corner, they turned and rode to the middle of the block where they guided their horses into an alley. After three blocks of riding in the dark alleys, they stopped at a corner and dismounted. A two-story hotel was a block up the street, its front window dimly lit. The only other light came from a full moon. No other horses were tied to hitching rails on the street.

For over thirty minutes nothing happened.

"That whore, she lied to me."

"Not a hell of a lot we can do about it," Jesse said, stroking the ears of his motionless horse.

"I'm going to keep my promise."

"Kill a woman?"

"When I make a promise, I keep it."

Abruptly, Billy put his finger to his lips. A man had stepped around the corner a block down on their side of the street. Billy and Jesse didn't move.

"Got to be Gonzales. When he gets here, right here," Billy whispered and pointed to the building's corner, "you take him with your gun out. I'll cover."

The man headed toward them and even in the silence of the night made no noise as he walked along the dirt street. Billy was certain it was Gonzales. Nobody else would be out that time of the night with a satchel. And even though it didn't rattle, it had to be full of gold coins.

When he was at the alley corner, Jesse stepped out with drawn gun. Billy remained behind him and to his side, in the shadows.

"I'll give you all the gold, don't shoot." It was said fast in English. Gonzales reached into the bag and spilled a handful of coins. His hand came out with a silver derringer. Two quick blasts followed from Billy's pistol. The first forty-one slug caught the dealer in the throat, the second, between his eyes, knocking his head back. He crumpled, dropping the small pistol and the leather satchel. Billy quickly picked it up before shoving his pistol into its holster. Grabbing the man's foot, he pulled him into the alley.

"Let's get out of here," Billy said, mounting up. "Head for the Rio Conchos. Riding slow, like we got no reason to be pounding out of town."

The two rode away from the hotel till they turned on the first street heading east toward the river. Silent for minutes, they kept their horses walking.

"Somebody must have heard those shots," Jesse finally said after glancing backwards for the forth or fifth time.

Billy nodded and shrugged. "They're used to gunshots."

No lights were on in the buildings they passed while the street was deserted with no horses at the hitching rails. Except for the sound of their horses' hoofs hitting the hard earth, there was no noise. They checked over their shoulders often, but no one was in sight. The buildings began to thin out alongside the road with only adobe shacks, small and dark, scattered among the mesquite and cedar trees.

With all the buildings behind them they were finally in the desert where the sandy road turned into wagon tracks, barely visible. Billy shoved the leather satchel into his saddlebag then spurred his horse into a smooth lope.

"The sonofabitch." Billy whacked his thigh with a clenched fist. "He'd still be alive, if he'd just paid up."

Both looked back, but nothing was moving.

"But hell," Billy said, "the sonofabitch needed killing."

"It's fifty miles to the Conchos River, northeast," Jesse said.

"Then we'll be there after sunup tomorrow, riding all day and most of the night."

"Yeah," Jesse said. "It's sixty more till Ojinaga on the big river. Then we'll cross into Texas."

"Buy some fresh horses in Ojinaga, if they got any good ones." Billy pulled his pistol, flipped the loading gate and pushed out the two empty cases. Taking two shells from his belt, he inserted them in the cylinder and slid the pistol into its holster.

"The Mexicans are thinking we'll head straight north, to Paso del Norte," Billy said.

For half an hour they rode along without talking.

"About back there." Jesse broke the silence.

"Yeah?"

"I owe you one, a big one."

"Maybe, maybe not. Things happen."

"No, I owe you."

"Jess, listen, let me tell you something."

"Give it to me."

"Okay, now listen. You know a lot about stealing and selling livestock."

The two swung their horses around a large clump of cholla cactus.

"Go on," Jesse said when they were again side by side.

"And you're good with a gun, Lloyd said. Fast and a good shot. Lloyd said you killed a Fletcher back in Las Cruces in a shootout."

"I put six bullets in the bastard."

"And he fired a full cylinder at you."

"Yeah, he was shooting and missing."

"That's the problem," Billy said.

"The problem? It was self-defense."

"That's not what I'm talking about." Billy slowed his horse so he could look directly at Jesse.

"You're saying what?"

"You don't know crap about gunfights, getting in the first shot, making it count before someone puts a slug in your gut. Someone shoots six times at you, you were just lucky."

"Maybe so, anyway like I said, I owe you a big one for back there."

"No, we're partners. That's what counts. We cover each other."

For minutes both rode is silence, guided by the sandy wagon tracks. In the west the moon was sliding down toward the horizon, the few lights from the town barely a dim glow. To the east the sky was taking on a lighter cast.

"Need to let the horses take a breather," Billy said, pulling up and slowly dismounting, the handle of his pistol glistening even in the fading moonlight.

6

Late August, 1877, Billy and Jesse had been back in Mesilla a month. They had stopped for several weeks in a Texas border town to help Billy's friend. He was in jail, accused of robbery. Billy and Jesse hung around until the sheriff was away on a trip, and then they broke the man out one night. They got the drop on the deputy who wanted nothing to do with two men with drawn guns. His friend rode off into west Texas.

Here in Mesilla, there was a group of men, myself included, who stole horses and cattle from down in Mexico and sold the livestock to ranchers on the Texas side. John Kinney figured out what ranches south of the border to raid and Jesse led the gang. Kinney owned a butcher shop in Mesilla where he sold mostly stolen beef, and ran a small ranch south of town. The group of men, referred to as The Boys, was a loosely connected bunch with men coming in and dropping out. Three of the regulars were Jim McDaniels, William Morton, and Frank Baker. Billy gambled a lot, but rode with us some times, never really fitting in being four or five years younger than the rest of us. By this time Billy was often referred to as The Kid because he didn't look very old. Here, he had not been in any gunfights, and Jesse and I never talked about the earlier shootings because we knew he was still wanted over in Arizona Territory for killing Cahill. Billy was friendly, but he was a loner.

By September, the group was talking about heading over to the Pecos area where trouble was brewing. On one side were Alex McSween and John Tunstall, merchants in Lincoln. They were supported by the cattle king, John Chisum, who ran cattle for hundreds of miles along the Pecos. Opposing this faction were the small ranchers who were backed by Lawrence Murphy and James Dolan, and also some small merchants in Lincoln. It was believed by many that Murphy and Dolan were backed by T.B. Catron, United States attorney for the Territory, a well-known lawyer who resided in Santa Fe and an owner of a large herd of cattle located north of Tularosa.

Selling beef to the Indian agencies and supplies to Fort Stanton, a U.S. Army post ten miles from Lincoln, involved big money. Both groups wanted to control this commerce. Lloyd

In Mesilla Jim McDaniels sat with Frank Baker and Jesse Evans at a table in the Overland Bar. Located in an adobe building that had been the station for the Butterfield Overland Stage back in the fifties, the bar was where The Boys hung out. Lloyd was tending bar since the regular barman was home with a sick wife. It was close to midnight. They had been drinking Pike's Magnolia whiskey for several hours. They were talking about going over to the Pecos River Valley when William Morton, John Kinney, and a well-dressed stranger walked in.

"Name's Baxter." The man sat down at the table.

"From Santa Fe," added Kinney, who like Baxter was also wearing city clothes.

Lloyd set three new glasses on the table and filled them.

"Kinney tells me you men might be heading to Lincoln."

"Yeah, maybe," Jesse said.

"Makes no difference to me," Baxter said. "But there's a lot of cattle to be had if you got the nerve."

"That right?" Jesse said.

Baxter looked around the table.

"How do you fit in?" Jesse asked. "Maybe we're interested and maybe we're not."

"Let's cut the bullshit, put our cards on the table face-up," Baxter said. He opened his coat, showing he was not armed.

"Go on," Jesse said.

"There's a powerful group of men in Santa Fe backing Murphy and Dolan."

"Catron?" Jesse asked.

Baxter took a drink from his glass and slowly, deliberately, set it back on the table.

"I want to know where we stand," Jesse said.

"These men, Murphy and Dolan," Baxter continued, "are willing to pay top dollar for unclaimed cattle. And there's thousands of head up and down the Pecos. Chisum's."

"The man is telling it like it is," Kinney said.

"Yeah?" Jesse interjected. "Well, I'd heard that too. Nothing new there. Not a thing I ain't heard before. An idiot can cut into Chisum's 'Jingle Bob' earmark and rework his 'Long Rail' brand."

"That's true," Baxter said. "And his cowboys can't cover all his spread-out cattle."

"Then what?" Jesse persisted.

"All you got to do is push a herd into Fort Stanton or the Indian agency," Baxter said. "You'll get paid. No questions asked."

"And the law?" Someone wanted to know.

"The men in Santa Fe will handle the sheriff and the law. And that's a commitment. And that part is new."

"We work for us," Jesse said.

"That's fine, the money is there. You'll get your share." Again Baxter picked up his glass, emptying it.

"We'll talk it over," Kinney said.

"You do that." Baxter stood and looked around the table then picked up his Stetson. "I've said all I've got to say." He shoved his hat on and walked out the door.

For a while the five sitting at the table remained silent, drinking, getting their glasses refilled. When Kinney remained silent, the others turned to face him.

"I know Baxter," Kinney said. "He's important, known in Santa Fe but not by the public. He sets things up, the others get their names in the papers. You can trust him."

Jesse looked around the table. "Kinney's word is good enough for me. At least it has been so far. When I come up from Texas in '72, Chisum hired me. I know how he handles his herds. Running off a couple hundred ain't going to be that hard."

They sat there for several minutes, no one else saying anything. Several smoked Bull Durham cigarettes, the smoke drifting up to the high viga-supported ceiling. The dim light from the hanging coal oil lamp made hazy, flickering shadows on the men's faces under their hat brims.

Jesse broke the silence. "Let's go to where the money is."

"Might as well," Baker said.

"Anybody else got something to say?" Kinney asked, but no one spoke out. "Okay, me and Morton will go over to the Rio Grand Hotel, tell Baxter."

After the two left, the three ordered another round. They were silent as their glasses were filled.

"We got to make up our minds about The Kid before we go," Baker said.

"What're you talking about?" Jesse asked.

"We want to know who The Kid is," McDaniels added. "He's been here a month and I still don't know what to think of him."

"He rubs me the wrong way," Baker said. "He could be working for one of the ranchers in the valley. For stealing horses you can get hung around here."

"He's a buddy of mine," Jesse said. "A good one."

"Yeah? But I don't like his looks, always smiling, whistling," Baker said.

"He ain't caused any trouble," Jesse said.

"Well, how long you knowed him?" Baker asked.

"Three, four months, since I met him at Camp Grant."

"What'd he do there?"

"He gambled, dealt mostly. Just like here."

"That don't mean nothing," Baker said. "Plus how do we know we can count on him if things get hot. He's a kid like Jim says."

"Hey, Lloyd," McDaniels yelled, "bring over that bottle of Magnolia."

"You can count on The Kid when the shooting starts," Jesse said. "I'll guarantee."

"Yeah," Baker said. "How do you know that?"

"I said it once, I ain't going to repeat myself."

"Could be I ought to just plug him," Baker said, "because maybe he's on our side and maybe he ain't."

"You can try," Jesse said.

"You saying I can't outshoot a kid?" He squared around to face Jess.

Jesse shoved his chair back from the table, clearing his holstered gun.

"Hold it," McDaniels yelled looking directly at Baker. "Jess here said The Kid's okay. That's good enough for me. He's the auger, and he's never led us down the wrong trail."

Baker emptied his glass and refilled it. He glowered at Jesse then laughed. "Whatever you say. That suits me. Hell, I ain't in the mood to kill some kid anyway."

"Fine, that's settled," McDaniels said. "What we need to talk about is moving over to the Pecos."

Baker reached over and grabbed the bottle, filling his glass halfway. Jesse kept his eyes on Baker and didn't move his chair back to the table.

7

Diary, page 18

All was settled. The Boys rode out in mid-October for the Pecos Valley. It had been fixed up for them to side with the Murphy-Dolan group. John Kinney stayed in Mesilla to take care of his ranch and butcher shop, and keep in touch with Baxter he said. But the fact was he didn't like sleeping on the ground. He was really a city boy. Another thing had changed. The word was out, The Kid was a killer, fast and accurate with his pistol. Who talked, I don't know whether it was Jesse trying to straighten out Baker, or someone from Arizona Territory—one of the many that Baker had dealt with selling stolen livestock. When Billy walked into a room there was that feeling I'd had before, bullets might start whistling by. So me, I did what I thought best, stayed in Mesilla. Lloyd

Frank Baker, William Morton, Jim McDaniels, Jesse, and The Kid squatted around a fire on the ranch, as it was now called, owned by the Murphy-Dolan Company. Located twenty miles southwest of Lincoln, it was on a stream that ran into Eagle Creek. The five had just pushed fifty head of cattle, all with the Chisum Jingle Bob ear cut, from a tributary of the Pecos thirty miles south of the Bosque Grande to this small ranch where there were no buildings, just tents. One old Mexican man did the cooking—pinto beans and beef. The new cattle were kept separated from the several hundred head that had ears already healed after having the Jingle Bob cut flat. These were held in a small canyon, ready to be delivered to the Mescalaro Reservation when the word was given. In early November a cold wind with snow flurries was blowing off the Sacramento Mountains. Sierra Blanca, jutting into the gray sky, was white with snow.

"Lloyd made the right decision heading back to Mesilla," Baker said. "It's a cold sonofabitch, riding all night facing that wind."

"Nobody was out, none of Chisum's men," Jesse said, "We didn't get shot at."

"Only nobody with no sense would be out."

"Quit bitching," Jesse said. "You got more money in your pocket than you ever had before."

Baker stood and kicked a large juniper log on the fire, stirring up smoke, ashes and sparks, the wind blowing all of it toward Jesse and The Kid.

Jesse stood yanking off his right-hand glove.

Baker remained motionless, arms and gloved hands hanging down.

Neither moved.

"You're asking for it," The Kid said as he slowly stood, turned his back and walked over to the horses. He never glanced back at Baker as he took a bucket full of corn and poured it into the trough in front of his horse.

"Okay," Jesse said. "I guess we're all tired, riding all night. Let's eat."

"Maybe The Kid and I want to finish it now," Baker said.

"I'll say when there's going to be gunplay," Jesse said, hand still close to his holstered pistol.

"Anytime." Billy, rubbing his horse's ears, turned and grinned at Baker. "Anytime."

Baker, still not removing his gloves, looked at Billy but said nothing else. He spun around and walked over to the large kettle of beans and beef hanging over a fire. The cook scooped out a dipper of the hash, filled a tin plate, and handed it to him. The others gathered around the large pot with their plates.

All except Billy who started rubbing down his big gray horse's back. He had ridden point and been the first to reach camp. The gray was a fine horse. Billy stroked his nose softly. That bullshitting Baker, mouthing off and keeping his gloves on. The big fake. Everyone knew he wouldn't try anything with his hands covered. But sooner or later, Billy figured, he would put a slug in Baker. If he had drawn on Jesse moments ago, gloves or not, he would've gotten another hole in his nose.

Several Mexican men rode up and dismounted. They were going to work on the Chisum brand—make an arrow out of the long bar and slice off the flap of the Jingle Bob ear-cut of the new cattle. The two Mexicans filled their plates with hash and cups with hot coffee. While the others were eating, Billy pulled his Winchester 73 carbine from its saddle boot, sat down on a stump, and wiped the rifle carefully with an oily rag, removing any drops of moisture. He jerked the lever several times, wiping the open chamber. Uncocking the hammer carefully, he slid the ejected shell back into the magazine. When finished he shoved the rifle back into the leather boot and eased his pistol from its holster. He wiped it with the rag, ejecting all the cartages. With a small rod he shoved a strip torn from the rag down the barrel, pulling it out the opposite end. Billy looked over at Baker and grinned. After reloading, he dropped the pistol into its holster and snapped the leather catch string over the hammer. He stood and walked slowly over to the pot, passing close to Baker but never looking at him again.

8

Memoir, page 1

I started writing this memoir mainly to tell about a period of time when Billy The Kid was involved in the war between the McSween-Tunstall faction and the Dolan-Murphy bunch and afterwards.

November of '77 was a cold month in Lincoln, with the smell of juniper smoke rising from the chimneys in every building. Mr. and Mrs. Alexander McSween had been living here since 1875 when they moved from Atchison, Kansas, after getting married. McSween had been having health problems and needed to live in a dryer climate. In Lincoln they were a well-known couple and lived in the finest house in town. Mrs. McSween ran the McSween-Turstall mercantile store that competed with the Murphy-Dolan business. In '77, wagon loads of merchandise from St. Louis arrived for her store. She was the one who seemed to make all the family and business decisions, always telling Mr. McSween what to do. She dressed formally, more so than any other woman in Lincoln, and acted very proper. Yet, there were rumors going around Lincoln about Mrs. McSween. Some whispered that she passed out her favors to lonely cowboys when her husband was out of town. All of this was said quietly, and never when McSween was around. Still, no one really knew for sure.

McSween's legal business was doing well in Lincoln, even though his biggest client, the Murphy-Dolan Company Store, had broken off with him. McSween would not defend some rustlers who worked for Murphy-Dolan. Everyone knew they were guilty. When the lawyer was fired by Murphy, Chisum hired him to prosecute the cattle thieves and he secured a conviction. McSween and Tunstall had also opened their mercantile business about that time. That's when the real trouble that finally led to bloodshed started in Lincoln.

Billy on big gray, his favorite horse, rode west through Lincoln along the mile-long single street lined with cottonwood trees. The rushing waters of the Rio Bonito were audible as it flowed eastward on the north side of town. On the southwest horizon a white-peaked Sierra Blanca protruded into the cloudy sky. Whistling softly, Billy was glad to get away from the Dolan cattle camp. Stealing livestock was not something he was really enthusiastic about, and as far as the money went he could take it or leave it. What he liked was sitting in a bar dealing cards, laughing and having a good time. The thing was, in life it seemed like everyplace you went it was necessary to choose one side or the other. Shooting someone was not a problem—everybody he'd shot needed killing. What was bothering Billy was that he didn't want to be told who needed to be shot. Stealing Chisum's cattle wasn't a concern, but killing one of his cowboys in the process, if it came to that, wasn't something Billy was happy about. The truth of the matter was Billy just didn't want to be bossed around, especially if shooting was part of the job.

In the early afternoon, the sun occasionally broke through the scattered clouds and felt warm on Billy's side although the cold west wind was biting. He was going to buy some wool trousers and maybe a wool shirt or two. His horse trotted past the Murphy-Dolan store, a large adobe and the only two-story house in Lincoln. Next door was the Sam Wortley Hotel and café. Billy pulled the gray up to watch a man in front of the mercantile store unhitch and feed a customer's horses while their owner was inside buying supplies.

The hell with Murphy-Dolan and their big business. Billy was going on down the street to the newly opened McSween store. If anyone didn't like it, let them try to do something about it. He hadn't met the McSweens and wondered what kind of people they were. Suppose they were honest, a concept he hadn't thought about much. One thing for sure, Billy had never heard anyone claim they were dishonest. So what if they were honest? Maybe it meant something, maybe it didn't.

Billy opened the store's door and walked in. On the left side, hanging on wooden wall pegs, were leather harnesses, coiled ropes, bridles with shiny bits and, on sawhorses, saddles. Groceries, coffee, bacon, tobacco, and cans of beans were on the opposite side. In the back, women's clothes hung on racks. In the middle were the men's clothes. With clouds covering the sun and no hanging lamp lit, the room was dim. An attractive woman stepped from behind a counter.

"Hello," she said.

Off came Billy's hat.

"I haven't seen you before." She walked forward, her long white dress with a full bustle rustling. "You must be new."

"Yes, ma'am, I am."

"I'm Mrs. Alexander McSween." She stepped closer. "How can I help you?"

"I need a thing or two." Her perfume was sweet and musky, her eyes gray, eyelashes dark and long. Her vivid red hair was pulled back in a cluster of ringlets with not a swirl out of place. Billy ran a hand through his shaggy hair, pushing it back while glancing down at muddy boots and ragged Levis.

"And what would that be, the thing you need?" She leaned her hip against a counter, one hand caressing a stack of coveralls.

"A wool shirt, some trousers."

"We certainly have those."

When she picked up a black wool shirt giving it a shake, he placed his hat on a counter. She held the shirt up checking the arm seams against Billy's shoulders. "A little large, but looks like a small will do it."

"I'll take two," Billy said.

"And trousers. You really have a narrow waist. Must be a twenty-six." She unfolded a pair of trousers and held them up to the side of Billy's waist, the pant legs just covering his booted ankles. "Seems just right to me."

"Okay." Billy stared at her, wondering what it would feel like to be dressed like that—a tight bodice, full petticoats, and long skirt. A way Billy had never dressed, not in Silver nor anyplace else. Plus, the woman knew she was attractive, which gave her lots of self confidence and an ability to deal with men on her terms, Billy was sure.

"In this cold weather you need things to keep you warm." She smiled, showing even rows of especially white teeth.

He handed her a twenty-dollar gold piece.

"There's nothing else you need?" she asked, leaning toward him. "Nothing I can help you with?"

"No, ma'am."

"How about a scarf? One to match those blue, blue eyes of yours." She picked up a large blue and white bandana. "This one would look real nice with that new black shirt."

"Yes, ma'am, that would be fine." Billy stepped back allowing her to walk past very close and go behind the counter.

"You haven't even told me your name," she said handing him dollar bills and a silver half-dollar in change.

"Billy. Billy Bonney."

"Billy, it's nice to meet you. Are you sure there is nothing else you need? Something I can get for you."

"No, ma'am."

"Well Billy, you certainly don't need a razor. I doubt you're old enough to shave."

"Oh, I shave now and again."

She laughed. "It doesn't look that way. You have nice skin, almost like a woman's."

"Pleased to have met you." Billy picked up his package, backing up several steps ready to leave.

"Likewise," she said. "You must just be passing through?"

"No, I'm here for a while."

"And who do you work for? Maybe Mr. Chisum?" she asked. "Neither Mr. McSween nor Mr. Tunstall have hired any new hands, although we could certainly use some."

"I work for myself."

"Yourself?" She looked at him, her hands pressing down on the counter, body leaning forward. She was no longer smiling. Her smoky eyes never looked away from Billy.

"Yes, ma'am. That's it."

"Now that does sound strange. A young cowboy working for himself."

Billy hesitated, looked over the store at the candy sticks, at skinny bottles of green pepper sauce, out the window. Finally Billy pulled out a pack of Bull Durham and turned toward her, staring into the eyes that were no longer smiling. He rolled a cigarette and lit it with a match swiped on the bottom of his boot.

"I do work for myself," Billy said. "Only myself."

She remained silent, as though waiting.

"I do jobs for Murphy-Dolan."

"Murphy-Dolan? I should have figured." She eyed the low-slung pistol. "Mr. McSween never even carries a gun. He was a Presbyterian minister."

"I didn't know."

"You know they're dishonest, thieves, Murphy-Dolan."

Billy said nothing.

"Why are you here? In this store? They have one down the street."

"I really don't know." He dropped the cigarette into a spittoon.

She remained behind the counter, standing stiffly with arms crossed.

"Mrs. McSween," Billy said, "I'm glad I came in here, talked to you."

"I don't know why, you're certainly not on our side."

Billy turned to leave but paused then spun around.

She had not moved, arms remaining crossed.

"At this moment, no," Billy said facing her, not smiling. He opened the door and stepped out.

9

1877 November

Leaving Lincoln behind and heading for Fort Sumner, Billy rode north slowly along the edge of the Pecos River Valley in grama grass up to the horse's belly. The purpose of the trip was to check out John Chisum's cattle that ranged along the river from Fort Sumner down to the Texas border. It was going to be a long ride, over a hundred miles, but that suited him fine. It was a bright sunny blue-sky day, with little wind. Billy whistled softly enjoying being away from the others, although riding around with Jesse was fun when it was just the two of them. And with a pistol, he'd practice putting holes in the center of a barrel cactus or two. Sometimes he liked to gallop along, slide to the side of the big gray, a leg hooked on the saddle, and fire from under the horse's neck. Jesse always laughed at him firing away, but his friend also had a lot of respect for Billy's gun-handling ability. Since the shooting of the dealer down in Chihuahua, his friend always stood by his side, especially when Baker acted up.

As Billy rode along glancing at the cattle along the Pecos, he admitted to himself that the thought of stealing Chisum's cattle was starting to bother him more than it had in the past. Pulling in an unbranded maverick or two was one thing. Rustling on a large scale like they had been doing was something else. Just two days ago, Billy and The Boys had delivered two hundred cattle at five bucks a head to the Mescalero Indian Agency. His cut of two hundred dollars, in gold coins, was in a small leather pouch shoved into his pocket. The feel of the hard gold coins against his leg would have been even better if the cattle-rustling hadn't started causing him those troubling thoughts—partly brought on by that conversation with the McSween woman.

Bought from the Army by the Maxwell family, Fort Sumner had a few saloons and a store or two. Several of its buildings were now used as a ranch headquarters by Pete Maxwell. Billy wanted to do some gambling there. Cowboys working for small ranches—started by men who had moved north from Texas—rode into Fort Sumner for an evening of drinking, dancing, and gambling. Chisum's men also came into town for the same reasons. The Mexicans who worked the fields and tended their goats generally stayed out of the bars. Still all in all, Billy figured there ought to be some card action.

Five days later, just after sundown, Billy stopped in front of a small stable in Fort Sumner and paid the man for keeping the big gray overnight. He slapped his hat against his leg, knocking dust from his trousers as well as from the hat. It had been a long ride. He walked down the street to Beaver Smith's Saloon. Half a dozen horses were tied to the hitching post, none with a long slash, Chisum's brand.

Behind the bar stood a tall, dark man with a large mustache. "What you having?"

"A beer."

The man grabbed a large brown bottle, twisted off the wire holding the cork in and shoved the beer with foam bubbling out in front of Billy.

"Ride a long way?' the man asked quietly, pulling his lips back slightly, not exactly smiling nor quite frowning, looking Billy over from his waist to his hat brim.

"Yeah." He took a small drink of the beer and looked around. Three cowboys stood at the bar and four sat at a table playing five-card stud. One kerosene lantern sat on a shelf behind the bar with another hanging from a ceiling beam. Billy looked back at the tall bartender who was filling a glass with whiskey. The man had the blackest eyes of anyone Billy could remember—except those of an Indian. Beneath his full mustache his teeth were white but slightly uneven. He was handsome and looked rugged like he could handle any trouble that might come up.

Billy drank slowly as he watched the bartender move like a big cougar going from one end of the counter to the other. One of the cowboys at the bar called out to him, "Pat, hey Pat, how about another shot of that Anchor whiskey?"

The bartender obliged him, as well as the other two standing by his side. He walked over to the card players' table and refilled their glasses, collecting from each as he went along. Finished with the others, he stopped in front of Billy and leaned on the bar, his face only inches away.

"You're new around here so I'll just say, you riding for Chisum this is the wrong bar," Pat said.

"If I'm not?"

"All these men work for the small ranchers. Chisum's men go to the White Owl Saloon up the street. They don't mingle."

"Thing is I ain't looking for trouble. But I don't back away either."

"Cowboy, let me tell you something. If you're not a Chisum man, you got no problem."

"Bonney, the name's Billy Bonney. I don't ride for Chisum."

"Pat Garrett." He stuck out his hand. "Hell, have another beer on me." Pat smiled. Even the black eyes seemed to relax when he grabbed another brown bottle and twisted the wire off, sliding it in front of Billy. His hands, with well defined veins, were broad and brown with long wide fingers that could certainly handle that big forty-four hanging from his waist in a well-used, brown leather holster.

"What I'm looking for is a card game."

"Hey, Tip," Pat called to one of the card players, "here's a new man, he's okay and looking to play cards."

Billy walked over and dropped a gold coin on the table. Tip pushed over two stacks of chips.

By one o'clock in the morning all the other cowboys had left. Pat and Billy sat at a table playing three-card Monte with Billy dealing. For over an hour it had been just the two of them.

"We close about this time," Pat said. "The cowboys are up at daybreak."

Billy turned over a heart, and Pat raked in two chips.

"I used to work for Chisum," Pat said.

Billy leaned back, placed the deck of cards on the table top and drank from a metal coffee mug. It seemed to Billy that the man across the table was more interested in talking than in playing.

"What happened?" Billy asked.

"Me and John did things different. He had his way while I had mine, but he was the boss, so I quit."

"I just rode in from Lincoln, all I ever saw was the Jingle Bob ear cut."

"John Chisum is a good man, but he wants to own everything from here to the Texas border. Which don't bother me. But it does the men with the little spreads."

"Most of the small ranchers here, they like the ones down in Seven Rivers next to the Texas border?"

"You could say that. A cowboy with no money comes up from Texas, stakes out a canyon, builds a cabin. First thing you know he's got twenty, thirty head. Those cattle come from only one place, Chisum's herds."

Billy picked up the cards and gave them a ripple.

"But the cowhands from the small outfits come into my place, say on Chisum's roundups he pulls in their cattle, ignores the brand. They ain't happy about that." Pat looked down watching Billy fan out the cards with a smooth fluid motion.

Billy glanced at Pat's face, at the black, black eyes, but quickly turned away when he looked up.

"But hell, there's always things to be said on both sides." Pat stretched out his long legs to the side of the table and shoved his holstered pistol around so the handle didn't jab into his hip. Now its barrel hung between his legs.

"Pat, you're a helluva tall man."

"The Mexicans here call me Juan Largo." Pat smiled his half-smile.

"Long John." Billy glanced down at Pat's pistol.

"I married Juanita Gutierrez. Long John, that's what she calls me."

"Seems like it fits."

"We've only been hitched for a month."

"Lots of my friends married Mexican women."

"They're around and available." Pat stood and stretched his big frame, his arms held high almost touching the viga ceiling. "Guess it's time to be closing up."

Billy finished his coffee, setting the mug back on the table, quietly.

"There's no hotel here, but you're welcome to throw your rigging on our front porch for tonight," Pat said. "Tomorrow is Saturday, more cowboys in town. Give you a chance to get up a bigger card game."

"Thanks, but I fixed things up to sleep at the stable."

"Come over midmorning, we'll have breakfast," Pat said. "Last house on the left, two blocks down."

Outside, Billy walked down the dirt street toward the stable, glancing back at Pat ambling down the middle of the street, headed home to his wife. Most men Billy met who carried a pistol, and that was almost everyone, Billy figured on outdrawing and out-shooting, if it came to that. There was usually a feeling of wanting to give it a try. But not with Pat. There was no itching to have a shooting match with him. Something else was working that was totally different.

Billy was attracted to this rugged, good-looking man. Thinking back to how it felt with the boy in Silver, and how it felt lying next to Jesse in the hotel room, this attraction was different. More intense and not just physical as it had been with Jesse and the boy.

Billy and Pat sat a table in the kitchen of a two-room adobe house, both eating eggs and bacon.

"This here is Apolinaria, my sister-in-law," Pat said, nodding at the woman placing extra bacon in a skillet on the wood stove. "My wife has been feeling poorly."

The woman poured more coffee into their cups.

"I don't open up the bar till the afternoon. Hardly any business before then." It was almost midday and Pat looked like he'd just gotten up.

Billy glanced across the table but kept on eating. It was his first full meal for almost a week. "Good bacon," he said.

"I own a hog farm," Pat said. "We raise our own meat. With the cold weather, just finished butchering several hogs. Tip, the guy you played cards with, runs the farm for me."

Apolinaria carried a plate of biscuits and a glass of milk through a door into a room where a woman lay on a bed, the covers pulled up to her neck.

"You think there's going to be trouble down in Lincoln between Dolan and McSween?" Pat asked, raking a biscuit across his plate, collecting bits and pieces of bacon and eggs. "You did say you were from Lincoln?"

"I am, and yeah, I do. Maybe shooting trouble, maybe not."

"Chisum is going to side with McSween and Tunstall," Pat said.

"I don't know how it's going to happen, what will start it, but I think you're right."

"Even here, like I said last night, things are real touchy between the small ranchers and Chisum. And I think it's going to end in gunplay."

"Could be." Billy stood. "Thanks for the breakfast."

"Only time I get any news is when some cowboy rides through."

A young attractive Mexican woman knocked briefly on the door and walked in.

"Buenos dias," she said and smiled at Billy.

"Celsa Gutierrez," Pat said.

"Mucho gusto," Billy said.

"Glad to meet you too," she said in English, again smiling at Billy. Turning to Pat she asked, "How's Mrs. Garrett?"

"Not eating much, still feeling poorly."

"Can I do anything?"

"No. Apolinaria is taking care of things."

"I'll be going," Billy said. "Need to buy me some tobacco."

"I work at the store," Celsa said. "I'll walk you there, it's three blocks over."

"You speak Spanish really good, like a native," Celsa said after Billy bought a sack of Bull Duram. "You work here?"

"No, just passing through."

"Too bad."

"Too bad?" Billy looked at her.

"You got pretty eyes." She laughed, showing small white teeth. "The next time you come through, stop at the store. I'll be there." She turned but looked over her shoulder at Billy, "You be sure and stop by."

Early Monday Billy rode south out of Fort Sumner, thinking about Pat, how rugged and handsome he was and how he seemed to know it. From the number of Mexican women who stopped at his house, Billy knew they too were aware of his good looks and raw natural charm. Sunday Billy had eaten breakfast with Pat again and, during the morning, three Mexican women stopped by to ask about his wife. All stayed awhile to talk with the tall man. The woman who remained the longest, making eyes at both Pat and Billy, was a handsome, dark, woman, Deluvina Maxwell. When she left, Pat said she had been a Navajo slave to his good friend Pete Maxwell and had taken on his name.

As the horse trotted along, Billy checked his Winchester, making sure it was secure in the boot. Saturday night he had played cards, winning about twenty dollars. The cowboys working for the small ranchers didn't have much money. After all the others had left, he and Pat had talked until almost two o'clock, with the tall man doing most of it. Pat had been a buffalo hunter up around Fort Griffin, or Hide Town as it was sometimes called. It was about 300 miles northwest of the town of Ft. Worth. A lot of shooting and fighting had gone on there. What killed the town though, Pat said, was that the hunters had wiped out most of the buffalo. That was when he'd quit and settled in Fort Sumner and gotten married.

A lot of their talk had been about the Lincoln situation and how Chisum was going to react. It was common knowledge that the Dolan bunch was stealing cattle, Pat said. But one thing stood out—Pat kept up on things and knew a lot about the situation along the Pecos even if he was just a bystander. But in all their talking, he had never asked where Billy fit in.

Thoughts drifted through Billy's head as the horse slowed to a walk. The sun was several notches above the horizon and felt warm. As to fitting in around Lincoln Town, that question was still unanswered. Which side to back? But there was one thing Billy's mind was made up about—a visit to McSween and Tunstall. Decide which way to face. And maybe the tall, black-eyed man would fit someplace in those plans. She couldn't stop thinking about Pat.

10

Memoir, page 6

The mercantile store of Alexander McSween and John Tunstall was doing well, cutting into the business of Murphy-Dolan. The Santa Fe Ring was not happy about this, especially its leader Thomas Benton Catron, United States District Attorney for the territory. It was rumored that the Murphy store was financed by Catron. He certainly seemed to control the governor, Samuel B. Axtell

At the Murphy ranch, Baker, Morton, McDaniels, and Jesse were sitting around the fire in front of a tent when Billy rode up. He filled a tin cup with hot coffee from a pot hanging over the cluster of red coals.

"Hey, Kid," Jesse said, "how was the trip?"

Billy squatted, blowing across the top of the mug.

"Rustle a lot of cattle?" Baker asked.

"Seen a lot," Billy said, "south between Chisum's Bosque ranch and his Springs River place. Lots of hands, too."

"How about north?" Jesse asked.

"Not as many, spread out more." Billy sipped from the cup.

"Not as many hands either, I bet."

"No, not as many."

"Just a longer haul with the cattle," Jesse said.

"Let's go for the closer bunch. The cowboys ought not to worry us," Baker said. "Just let The Kid take care of Chisum's men."

Billy took a big swallow of coffee, set the cup down on a flat rock, and strode over to his horse. He eased the saddle and blanket off, placing them on a large boulder. He pulled the Winchester from its boot along with the oily rag. Back at the fire he sat down wiping the rifle slowly, carefully pointing it away from the other men. Billy swung the gun skyward, levered a shell into the chamber, sighted at a tree nearby, but didn't fire easing the hammer down slowly.

"Baker, whatever Jesse says, that's the way we do it."

During the time Billy was talking to the group at the Murphy ranch, Baxter and two other men, in an adobe building south of the Santa Fe Plaza, sat around a large table listening to James J. Dolan. Dolan had spent six days riding to discuss his problem with these men, the leaders of the Santa Fe Ring.

"Things are getting tense over on the Pecos," Dolan said, frowning.

"We've heard," Baxter said.

"The store business is hurting. That damn McSween is undercutting us."

"And the cattle business? What about it?" Baxter asked. "Supplying beef to Fort Stanton and the Mescalero Indian Agency."

"That's another problem. Chisum."

One of the men was heavyset, in a white shirt, black string tie, and matching black dress coat and trousers. He kept his eyes on Dolan but said nothing. In the light from the lamps mounted on the walls, his balding head gleamed, making his stingy gray hair seem even thinner. The other older man, dressed similarly, was not as heavyset. He smoked a cigarette taken from a tin box and remained silent.

"What about Chisum?" Baxter asked.

"Old John's riled up, getting his cattle stolen," Dolan said. "He's getting hit two ways. By us and by the small ranchers, mostly those located south of Seven Rivers. Up north around Fort Sumner, the boys with the small spreads are helping themselves to Chisum's cattle too."

"Hell, he's got close to ninety thousand head. How's he going to know when a hundred goes missing?" Baxter asked.

"Hiring more hands. He's got close to a hundred working for him."

"We got you the contracts at Fort Stanton and the Indian agency," the heavyset man said clipping the end off a fresh cigar with a small pair of silver scissors. "It's up to you to get the beef."

"That's not the only problem with Chisum," Dolan said.

"Go on," Baxter said.

"He's backing McSween and Tunstall in their other business, the Lincoln County Bank. They're undercutting us there too with loans to the farmers and small ranchers coming in to buy land."

"Sounds like you need to get things straightened out," the heavyset, cigar smoking man said.

"I need help, I can't do it all," Dolan said. "That's why I took two weeks off to come up here and see what you can do."

"How about the men I got from Mesilla a month ago, the Evans gang or The Boys as they were called in Mesilla?" Baxter said. "Are they getting it done or not?"

"They do okay, but it's getting harder to get the cattle."

"Hire additional men out of Mesilla. John Kinney's still got more," Baxter said. "In fact, I'll go down and enlist some, do it myself. Let them work with Evans."

"There's another problem. The store could go bankrupt. Since Riley and I bought out Murphy, we're out of cash," the cigar smoker said. "It appears to me that all this trouble started when that damn Englishman moved in and started financing the other store, started his ranch, and now a bank." He looked at Dolan, "Hell, you're an Irishman, you know how the English will move in and take over."

"That's about it," Dolan said.

"Maybe we ought to just get rid of Tunstall." The man took a heavy drag on his cigar and blew smoke into the air.

"Get rid of Tunstall?" The other well-dressed man spoke for the first time.

"One way or the other." The man removed his cigar and spit into a silver spittoon. "That's my money in that store. I fought on the losing side in one war, I don't intend to lose this one."

"How the hell did an officer in the Confederate army become such a staunch and successful Republican?" the other well-dressed man asked and smiled.

"I got tired of losing, besides that war is over. What we have to decide here is, how do we push McSween out of the way?"

"What about Tunstall?" Dolan asked. "He's the real problem, the man with the assets."

"Well, Dolan, I thought I'd leave John up to you and Sheriff Brady," the cigar smoker said. "I suppose he's still willing to do things for us?"

"He is." Dolan emphasized his remark by tapping the table with his index finger. "Remember me and him served at Fort Stanton together. I still buy his New Mexico scrip at face value. I got a drawer full. So, yeah, he's on our side, does mostly whatever we say."

"How does he feel about Tunstall?" He studied the cigar's end, the red ember.

"He's an Irishman too, from the County of Cavan where the English took all the land under their plantation system. Brady's been here twenty years, but he hasn't forgotten."

"So you and Brady can take care of Tunstall." The large man studied his cigar carefully. "We can count on it?"

"I need to be going," the other well-dressed man interrupted. "You boys do whatever is necessary as far as Tunstall is concerned. But my office does not want to be involved, will not be." He rose and walked into another room.

"That's just like him, doesn't want to get his hands dirty," the cigar smoker said. "From what I hear, it was the same when he was in the California gold fields. Certainly in Utah he tried to stay out of the line of fire, but didn't always succeed. Got labeled a Morman."

"Brady and me, you want us to take care of Tunstall? That's what I'm hearing. And McSween?" asked Dolan.

"McSween is still involved in court with the Fritz estate," Baxter said. "I'll get Fritz's brother and sister to file a complaint about not getting the ten thousand from the policy. Then we ought to be able to get an injunction against him. Take merchandise from his store, shut him down. That will hit Tunstall hard, his money is in that store. Then you do whatever to get Tunstall out of the picture. Permanently."

The cigar-smoking man picked up the liquor bottle and filled all the glasses. He looked at the almost empty decanter then at Dolan. "That's right, we need to do whatever is necessary. Here and in Lincoln. Particularly in Lincoln. Especially concerning Tunstall."

11

Billy saddled up ready to leave the cattle camp and ride into Lincoln. The others could herd a hundred head to Fort Stanton.

"Hey Kid, you ain't earning your pay," Baker said.

Billy mounted.

"Maybe I'll just take your cut," Baker said.

"Try it," Billy said, his hand resting lightly on his thigh.

Baker looked at him but said nothing else.

Mrs. Alexander McSween stepped from behind the counter to confront Billy, blocking his way when he entered the store.

"Well, if it isn't Billy Bonney," she said.

"Yes, ma'am." He removed his hat with his left hand.

"And what can I do for you this morning?"

"I stopped by to see Mr. McSween."

She looked down at his low-slung pistol, at his right hand that was level with his holster, and finally at the blue bandana around his neck.

"If he's here," Billy said.

"And if he's not?"

"I'll come back when it's convenient."

"Why do you men all walk around armed? It's not dangerous in the store."

"Mrs. McSween, I mean your husband no harm."

"You still ride with the Dolan gang?"

"The last time I was here we talked about that."

"Yes," she said, "we did." She took several steps toward Billy only stopping when she was within an arm's length. "And your business with my husband?"

"I want to meet him. Him and Mr. Tunstall. Talk to them."

"Talk. Well! Not threaten them?"

"I've thought about what you said, about Dolan. How I fit in."

"And what did you decide?"

"I'm still thinking on it. I didn't take what you said lightly."

Without moving she looked directly into the blue eyes.

"Your words, your opinion, they're important to me," Billy said.

"I see," she said still not looking away, still intense. "You do seem different today."

Billy nodded, having cleaned up, combed the dark brown hair, and put on the wool shirt bought the last time he was in the store.

"Maybe you're thinking differently too." She reached up and smoothed out a wrinkle in his bandana. Her bright red hair was pulled back in a swirl of curls the same as before, her perfume just as fragrant.

"I may look different," Billy said. "But you don't. You always dress so proper."

"I'm from Atchison, Kansas. A city-woman. We always dress this way and there most men don't have guns hanging on their waists. That frightens me. I've told that to Mr. McSween many times since we moved to Lincoln."

"It's a part of us out here." Billy's hand touched her arm softly, an intimate touch, as one woman might touch another, a close friend seeking to be understood. Billy had never done this before. In fact there had never been a girl or a woman for a friend.

Billy watched her face as she glanced down at the slender fingers on her forearm, wondering what she was thinking. Wanting to tell her. What? That the two had a lot in common even if they didn't dress alike? What Billy's real secret was?

"Another side of you is showing today," Mrs. McSween said. "A softer side. And I like it better, much better."

Slowly Billy's hand slid off her arm.

"Mr. McSween is in his office in the bank, the building attached to this store. He would talk with you, possibly it is something he would like doing."

"Yes, ma'am."

"Mr. McSween and Mr. Tunstall, with the help of Mr. Chisum, opened the Lincoln County Bank a month ago. Just walk in."

Billy nodded and turned to leave.

"Billy Bonney, old enough to carry a pistol but too young to shave." For the first time that morning she smiled when he glanced back before closing the door.

Alexander McSween stood when Billy walked into his office and stopped in front of his desk. For a moment's duration neither spoke nor moved. McSween, who was several inches taller than Billy, had a black drooping mustache, brown eyes, and long dark wavy hair combed straight back.

"Yes?" McSween remained behind his desk. He looked like a businessman, with white shirt, black jacket, and black string tie. Certainly not a rancher.

"Bonney." Billy did not remove his hat nor offer his hand.

Again, neither spoke.

"I wanted to meet you," Billy said.

"I've heard your name. I believe you ride with Jess Evans."

"I do."

Both men remained standing.

"I don't know what transaction you and I might conduct." Alexander ran his hand through his hair, ruffling it.

"I don't believe you are in the business of buying stolen cattle," Billy said.

"No, I'm not." He opened his coat to show he was unarmed. "There are two groups in town, one's honest, the other's not. One's nonviolent, the other's not."

"People say that."

Again Alexander ran his hand through his hair.

Billy sat down in one of the straight back-chairs in front of the desk.

"Bonney, why are you here?"

"To tell the truth, I'm not sure. But I'll give you a half answer."

Alexander sat down placing his hands on the top of his desk, interlacing fingers that were long, slender, slightly pink and looked very soft. Billy wanted to smile, for this man's movement seemed womanly, the way he touched his hair, clasped his fingers, and crossed his legs at the knee so deliberately.

"I know one faction, I wanted to meet the other," Billy said.

"Fair enough. Now I've met the other faction, Dolan, Riley, Jess Evans and gang, more than enough."

"Jesse is my friend."

"So I've heard." He placed his hands palm down on the polished desk, his manicured fingernails clean and cut evenly. "Not one of those men has bothered to stop by and visit, say hello. See if we can accommodate each other."

"This is the first bank I've been in."

"You've surprised me, dropping by."

"As I told Mrs. McSween, I wanted to meet you. She told me about the bank."

"Mr. Tunstall is the majority owner. If you want to meet the complete other side, you should meet John. He too is an honest man."

"And where would I meet John Tunstall?"

"The café in the Wortley Hotel." Alexander smiled. "Across the street from Dolan's. John has lunch there everyday when he's in town. One o'clock, promptly."

When Billy rose Alexander stood, hesitated, but reached out his hand, which Billy clasped. It was soft and smooth without calluses.

Billy was sitting at the café's counter when John Tunstall came in. They met in the center of the room and Tunstall immediately extended his hand.

"Mr. Bonney, I believe." He smiled.

"Most folks call me Billy."

"Alexander said you would be here."

A waitress led them over to a table by a window.

"My table," Tunstall said. "Have a seat."

After the waitress took their orders, she brought two cups of coffee.

"Dolan, Murphy, and I have talked on a number of occasions," Tunstall said, "always trying to be friendly. Not usually succeeding."

Billy didn't respond.

"I have not talked with or met Jess Evans or any of his crew, though I occasionally see them around town."

"I'm not here for Dolan or Murphy. Jesse is my friend, but I'm not here for him either."

"I didn't think you were." He unbuttoned his double-breasted gray woolen coat, displaying a holster and pistol. The holster was shiny brown leather, appearing new and not well used. "And you are the first to look me up when there wasn't a problem. So why are you here?"

"Fact of the matter is, Mr. Tunstall, I'm not sure why I'm here, why I even decided I wanted to meet you and your partner."

Tunstall pulled two cigars from his inside coat pocket and offered Billy one.

Billy shook his head, pulled out a sack of Bull Durham and rolled a cigarette.

Tunstall lit his cigar and the cigarette. He seemed small and thin in his large coat and, though he was brown from the sun, there was a paleness about his face.

"The two groups are trying to monopolize the trade with both the Indian Agency and the Army at Fort Stanton." He blew cigar smoke at the slit of the slightly raised window before looking back at Billy. "Both are trying to establish a store that will be the center of commerce in Lincoln. One or the other will succeed."

Billy glanced out the window when the waitress refilled their cups of coffee.

Slowly a grin spread across Tunstall's face. "Hell, for sure you're not here to listen to me argue about who is right or wrong."

Another woman placed plates with large steaks in front of them.

"But I do know why you're here," Tunstall said

Billy stopped cutting his meat and faced Tunstall directly.

"I crossed an ocean, left Canada, traveled three thousand miles over mountains and prairies to find a life I wanted to live."

Billy sat without moving, the knife clasped in his hand.

"I think it's the same for you. You're looking, just like I was."

"Maybe I am."

"The only difference is our age. I'm twenty-five. You're what? Eighteen, nineteen?"

"Eighteen."

"People like us, you, me, we start to dream at some point in our lives. Maybe even unaware of what is going on in our heads."

Carefully Billy placed the knife across his plate.

"I have a small ranch on the Rio Feliz. Dick Brewer is my foreman."

"I've seen him around," Billy said.

"I'd like for you to ride out to my place with Dick and me."

Billy sat without moving then leaned back in the chair, away from the table, his arms crossed.

"Don't take that the wrong way. I'm not asking you to switch sides. I'm not even asking you to consider it. I'd just like for us to talk, for you to meet Dick and see my place."

"I can do whatever I want to do," Billy said. "I can take care of myself. But I don't desert my friends easy."

"Jess Evans?"

"Yeah, Jess."

"That's a fine trait. An admirable one. Someday I hope to earn your friendship, but for now let's just move along. Don't make any decisions."

"I'm glad we met." Billy shoved his plate with the large steak to the center of the table and stood. "Talking with you and McSween, that was something I wanted to do."

Tunstall nodded and rose.

"I'm going to do a lot of thinking." Billy extended his hand and the Englishman grasped it, holding it firmly. "I'll see you in a day or two."

Outside Billy did not glance at the large adobe building across the street to see if anyone was watching. Unhitching the big gray, he swung into the saddle and rode slowly out of town.

12

At his small farm on the Rio Ruidoso, Dick Brewer was filling a water trough in an undersized corral holding a few head of cattle. A one-room log cabin sat back in the ponderosa pines. John Tunstall and Billy rode up, dismounted, and shook hands with Brewer. The men talked for several minutes then Dick saddled up and the three headed out to Tunstall's ranch on the Rio Feliz. Even though the sun was bright and the sky blue, it was a chilly day because of a cold north wind.

They rode down the one street that ran through the small community of San Patricio, now inhabited mostly by Hispanic farmers though initially it had been settled by Irish troopers discharged from the cavalry. Several people bundled in colorful wool serapes walked by, smiled, and waved at Dick.

"Seem like they know you," Billy said.

"They have fine bailes here, small but really good." Dick said. "You like to dance?"

"I do."

"One Saturday night we'll drop in. Lots of single Mexican woman."

Billy glanced at Dick who was a large man with thick shoulders and big hands. He was good looking with his curly dark blond hair, light blue eyes and cheeks rosy from the cold. He was almost too pretty but probably a favorite with the Mexican women. He seemed like a guy interested in having a good time.

How dancing with a woman would be, Billy didn't know. But she was a good dancer even if it was something she hadn't done in several years. Hell yes. Going to a baile would be fun, scooting across the dance floor in time with some fast music like Turkey in the Straw. Billy would just have to lead instead of follow.

Leaving the tiny village, they turned southeast and rode across open range until intersecting a well-used wagon trail leading due south. By late evening they had reached Tunstall's ranch house, a large square adobe building. In its open center were flowers and trees. Close by was a corral where they turned out their horses, placing the saddles in an adjacent barn.

Godfrey Gauss, the cook at the ranch, cut strips of meat from a hanging beef in the barn. He soon stoked up a roaring fire in the kitchen cook stove. Several coal oil lamps lit the kitchen while the meat sizzled in the skillet and a pot of beans bubbled on the back of the stove. Gauss served large platters of steak with beans on the side. All three men ate without saying much.

Afterwards, while Tunstall made a few statements about the country, the other two rolled cigarettes lighting them from the top of the chimney of a lamp. Billy, as usual, took several puffs then pitched the butt into the stove where a lid had been removed from its round opening. Though Dick occasionally emphasized some point, Tunstall did most of the talking—about starting a ranch, how the land was especially suitable for grazing cattle with plenty of grass and good water. Small parcels of land were still available cheap and there was lots of open range even if Chisum tried to control most of it in the Pecos Valley. But in the headwaters of the Rio Bonito and Ruidoso, there was lots of open range available if a beginning farmer-rancher bought a small parcel of land along the stream.

Gauss brought out a bottle of Scotch although Billy asked for more coffee. Dick poured a shot of liquor. Tunstall abstained. The three remained silent as Dick drank slowly, seeming to savor each sip.

Then Tunstall walked them through his home showing the eight or so rock chimneys and stoves. His bedroom had a large fireplace and a twelve-foot-long hearth. He was particularly proud of the building, Billy figured. Bear rugs were scattered throughout. When they had seen all the rooms, Billy and Dick went out to the bunkhouse and each took a small room.

The following morning was windless with a blue sky. Billy, Dick, and John Tunstall rode side by side heading north along the wagon trail. No one talked for several miles. They listened to the creaking of the cold saddle leather and watched the horses' breath, white plumes in the crisp mountain air.

Tunstall broke the silence. "Like I said, land is cheap. A young man can start a small place with a few head while working for a bigger rancher. It's an honest living, something a man can grow into. Just the way Dick is doing."

Dick nodded, adding nothing.

"I've got a big place, over a thousand acres not counting the adjacent open range. There's plenty of grass and water. The Feliz runs the year around. I've stocked my place with three to four hundred head."

The horses followed the wagon tracks without the men having to pull the reins to one side or the other except when an arroyo cut across the road.

"The problem is, cattle wander off, disappear."

"I do what I can," Dick said.

"He does. A number of times, with a small posse, he's chased down rustlers when he was out-numbered three or four to one. Brought the livestock back to my ranch."

Billy looked at Brewer, studying the way he sat his horse, the Winchester, its faded stock forward in a well worn saddle boot, the forty-five pistol strapped on his waist.

"But it's a long ride between his place and here. He's going to hire a couple more hands part-time to help out." Tunstall turned toward Billy. "What I need though is one good man to stay here all the time. Keep a watch on the cattle."

Billy shifted in the saddle to face Tunstall.

"I'll pay well, especially for someone who'll face the men taking the livestock. Someone who's not afraid if there's some gunplay. I'd also help the man start a small spread."

"I won't back down from men with guns," Billy said, "someone trying to steal cattle."

"I know that. That's why I'm offering you a job."

Billy pulled up his horse, slung his leg over the saddle horn, and studied the open range to the east, foot-tall grass as far as the eye could see, the sun a bright orange sphere slightly above the sea of yellow.

"I know it's a big decision for you," Tunstall said. "Take your time, think it over."

Billy nodded, still looking at the far horizon. It was the first offer for an honest job that had come along, the first offer to be someone someday. An offer from a man of position, someone who had not hesitated to shake hands or talk face to face, a man who evidently respected and trusted Billy. If this was what Billy wanted, to be a rancher.

If not, maybe he should just ride away, find a place where no one had heard of the killing in Silver. Perhaps down in south Texas. Let Bonney disappear. Pick another name, something other than Wilma like Wanda, dress like Mrs. McSween. Except right now Billy liked the way life was going. Riding with the men. Doing things on their terms in their world. It was something Billy had been doing since she had started riding a horse when she was six. Too, she didn't have the confidence of the McSween woman when it came to competing with other women, facing a man as a woman. So maybe for now she should give it a try, run a ranch, build up a small spread, and stay Billy.

But there was one thing she was going to do while staying Billy—visit and spend time with Mrs. McSween. Learn something about being a woman. That was important now, finding out how to behave around men, gaining the confidence exhibited by a woman who was sure of herself.

Billy turned from gazing at the Pecos Valley to face Tunstall. "Okay, I'll take the job."

"Just like that? I'm pleased."

Billy nodded, giving his nonchalant smile.

"You can start whenever you want."

"I'll need to go to Dolan's cattle camp, let Jesse and the others know."

Tunstall shifted his body in the saddle to study Billy's face, a slight frown on his.

"I have to do that, tell Jesse."

Without commenting, Tunstall nodded.

"You need someone to go with you?" Dick asked.

Billy turned to scrutinize Dick again. It was a courageous offer. They'd be out-gunned six or seven to one, what with the new men that had ridden in—some of The Boys who at first had stayed with Kinney. Dick might be too pretty, but it was all on the outside. He was a tough guy, unafraid. Billy was sure of that.

"No, I can handle it."

Tunstall had ridden on ahead.

"If you're sure."

"Thanks but this is about me, nothing else. It's up to me, my decision."

"Okay."

Billy pulled his horse around so he could face Dick directly. "It was a fine offer."

"Well, here's a different one. When you get some land for your spread, I'll help you get started."

"I figure I'll need help then and there."

Dick smiled. "While Tunstall can't hear, let me tell you about all us little guys. To get started we don't have the money to buy stock."

Billy shifted in his saddle but said nothing.

"We have to find some unbranded calves, mavericks. All of us do it. There's plenty around, mostly Chisum's. Like I said, I'll help you get started. We'll take a few cows too, just a few. Not hundreds like, well you know, like Dolan's bunch does."

"Yeah, okay."

13

Billy topped out on the small ridge overlooking the camp and pulled his horse up in the cedars and pinion. There they were, sixteen or seventeen men sitting and standing around a large fire on Dolan's cattle ranch. Some were new men. A few he recognized as part of the Kinney gang from back in Mesilla. Others were strangers. He had chosen to come in from the top of the ridge to look over the layout rather than riding in along the flat narrow valley. Several hundred yards up the canyon, in a large draw, was a herd of cattle, a hundred or so.

Slipping the leather holding loop from the hammer of his pistol, he nudged his horse forward, riding slowly down into the group. He stopped at its edge. Men were on both sides. He nodded at Jesse and looked over at Baker, Morton, and McDaniels. But his gaze returned to Jesse.

Billy didn't dismount. One hand held the reins tight. The other rested on his right thigh. He backed the big gray up several steps so that everyone was now in front of him.

"What's up?" Jesse asked, obviously aware Billy was going to say something, do something that was going to cause a problem.

Billy felt the need for a couple of quick puffs on a cigarette but resisted the urge, keeping his hand on his thigh.

Frank Baker stood up with most of the others, who stopped whatever they were doing and turned to face Billy.

"I took a job with John Tunstall."

Jesse stared at Billy, his smile fading yet no visible emotion replaced it.

"You did what?" Baker said.

"You heard me."

"Hell, you'll be shooting at us first chance you get," Baker said.

His hand remaining motionless, Billy kept his eyes moving to watch all of them but primarily he focused on Baker.

"We might as well start the party now," Baker said pulling his right glove off.

"Yeah, Baker, you bastard. You're ready when you got me outgunned."

"Let's do it," Baker said loudly to the men around him.

"If that's the way you want it. Have at it." Billy's hand didn't move, but his eyes bored into Baker.

"Hold it!" Jesse yelled even louder, squaring around to face Baker. His hand hung loosely at his side close to his pistol handle. "Just hold it."

Baker stood motionless.

"Billy's rode with us, fought with us, slept with us, done whatever we needed," Jesse said.

"He's gone to the other side," Baker said.

"Yeah, and he rode in here to tell us, face to face. Man to man. Not by letting us know with a forty-four slug from his Winchester whistling by."

Billy stroked the gray with his left hand, settling him. His right hand remained on his thigh.

"We let Billy ride out, just like he rode in. No trouble," Jesse said.

Baker spat at the ground. The other men remained motionless.

"Well, Billy, I guess that's it. Don't know when we'll see you again, but you're free to go." Jesse looked around then back at Billy.

Billy nodded, eased the reins to the right and slowly turned his horse to ride away down the canyon. He never looked back.

Two weeks later in early December, Brewer, Billy and Fred Waite, a Choctaw from the Indian Territory, arrived at the barn on Brewer's place. They worked six longhorn cows with the Jingle Bob ear-cut and two unbranded almost-grown calves into the small building. Fred, who Dick hired to work part time at Tunstall's place, and Billy had became good friends. They took care of their boss's cattle, mostly repairing corrals. Though Billy was six years younger, clearly the Choctaw looked up to him, impressed with his shooting and riding ability. The two had decided to go in together on a small spread along the Rio Ruidoso the following spring.

The men dismounted, pulling off their saddles and placing them on a top rail along one side of the barn. Billy pulled his Winchester and wiped it down with the oily rag, paying particular attention to the trigger and hammer. He shoved the rifle back into the boot.

"You love those guns like they was a woman," Fred said smiling.

"Yeah, they keep me alive. A woman wouldn't." Billy pulled his .41 Colt, cleaning it before taking a similar pistol from his saddlebag and oiling it.

"It was a cold ride, but we got the cattle without any trouble," Dick said. "I'll work over the brand here in the barn. I got a little corral up in the pines where I'll keep them till everything's healed. By Christmas I'll have the cows bred to my bull."

During a driving snow storm, the three men had herded the eight head up the Feliz River without seeing any of Chisum's hands. They had found fifty head up a small canyon close to the confluence of the Pecos and the Feliz. The three had stopped at the Tunstall ranch overnight then, at daylight the next morning, cut south on the open range bypassing San Patricio. With one man in the rear and one on each side, they had pushed the cattle hard to reach Dick's place by sundown.

In his small one-room cabin, Dick got a fire going in the cook-stove. The other two stood close by enjoying the heat after the hard forty-eight-hour ride in the snow storm. When the coffee pot, with a cup of dry coffee dumped into the water, started bubbling they filled tin mugs.

"Glad we didn't have a shooting scrap with Chisum's men," Fred said, both hands around his mug.

"If you go during a snowstorm, it turns out that way," Dick said bending over. He stirred up the logs with a poker stuck through the large round opening in the stove's top.

"I don't like shooting at working cowboys," Fred said.

"Shooting, sometimes it's necessary, sometimes no." Dick turned toward Billy. "About shooting. You take care when you ride into Lincoln for supplies. Everybody there knows you switched sides, including Brady, our good sheriff."

Billy shrugged. "I worked for him for several days on his ranch when I first came here. He won't draw against me. He likes living better than doing something foolish."

"Someday there's going to be a shooting," Dick said.

"Nobody is going to face me, not Brady and none of that Evans bunch."

"It's your back you got to watch." Dick threw some thick strips of bacon into a black skillet.

Billy smiled his usual the-hell-with-it smile. "Dick, what we got to do is head over to San Patricio this Saturday night. Do some dancing before I ride back to the ranch the next morning. Get you to introduce me to the señoritas. Take Fred with us."

Dick flipped the sizzling bacon. "We sure as hell can do that!"

14

Billy sat in the kitchen of Tunstall's ranch house finishing a big meal of steak and beans, drinking hot coffee. Gauss who spoke little and then with a heavy German accent, wiped out the skillet, hung it on a wall peg behind the stove and wandered off to another part of the house. That day, from sunup to past sundown, Billy had ridden from one end of the ranch to the other counting cattle, three hundred and eighty-six. Gauss had said that this was the first time the cattle had been tallied in months. Not since Tunstall had bid on and gotten two hundred head at a Sheriff's auction, made necessary when a small ranching family couldn't pay the taxes.

Billy refilled his mug, leaned back on two legs of the split pine chair and placed both boots on the long bench. He glanced out the window at the slice of moon. It had been a long day. But right now he wasn't thinking about the cattle or the tiring ride. Two weeks ago there had been thirty or forty people at the San Patricio baile on a night with a full moon. It had been clear but cold, making dancing to the fast tunes with the women fun. It had worked out fine. Besides meeting the women Dick introduced, he had got to know quite a few of the men. There was one in particular he liked, Charley Bowdre from Mississippi, who had a small farm on the Ruidoso. Charley Bowdre grew corn and vegetables to sell at Fort Stanton and ran a few head of cattle. He told Billy he was married to a Mexican woman, Manuela.

Billy smiled, thinking back. Manuela and Billy had spoken Spanish to each other, something Charley couldn't do. When she had asked him if he had Mexican blood, speaking Spanish so good, he'd laughed and said he didn't think so. With her hair piled on her head in rows of amber curls and hanging down her back in waves, and with her light complexion, she looked Anglo. But when Billy asked if she was—in spite of what Charley had said—she had laughed and said no, she was Spanish through and through.

The two had gotten along really fine, laughing a lot. At the next baile, she wanted to fix Billy up with one of the single women living in town. Billy blew across his mug and took a drink of the hot black coffee. Now that would be a problem. Dancing with a woman was okay, fun, especially to the fast music. But going back to a house, the situation could get awkward in a hurry. Just sticking to the dancing would be the thing to do. The big question though, the thought that was always popping up was how much longer Billy should continue the masquerade? There seemed no good answer. It was either keep things the way they were or ride away. Billy wasn't ready to leave, not yet. Anyway there was no hurry to do anything because in several days he was riding into Lincoln to talk to Tunstall about the cattle count and probably stay there for a week to get in some card playing.

A few days later, around midnight, Billy left his hotel room in the Sam Wortley hotel and entered the bar to find Tunstall and Garrett sitting at a table, with shots of whiskey in front of them. They motioned him over.

Pat explained he'd ridden into Lincoln to look things over, talk to some of the men in the two factions, try to figure out the way the wind was blowing. And his wife had died.

"I needed to get out of town, see some different country," Pat said.

"Sorry to hear about your wife," Tunstall said.

"She'd been feeling poorly for quite a spell, just couldn't get over it."

Billy studied Pat's face in the flickering light from the kerosene lamps and the fireplace where juniper wood burned and popped. He looked gaunt, his face tight, like he had been drinking steadily for some time. His black eyes seemed even blacker, his long fingers even longer and slimmer. The big holster with the .44 pistol rested on his thigh.

"What's your plans?" Billy asked.

"Right now I'm just thinking on things." He emptied his shot glass and signaled for a refill. "Anyway in life the wagon keeps rolling. We buried her three weeks ago."

"Maybe you ought to stay here in town for awhile," Billy said.

"Lincoln's okay, but I got to stay moving. Things to be done." He swirled the amber liquid in his glass and drank half before setting it back down slowly, deliberately.

"Playing cards, doing some betting, might be what you need," Billy said. "Staying in town here, doing that might help you get your mind off your troubles."

"I'd like to, but I just couldn't sit around."

"By the way, how's Celsa Gutierrez, that girl that works at the store? She still around?" Billy asked.

"Yeah, seen her several weeks ago, came around to help when my wife passed away."

"If we can be of any help whatsoever, let us know," Tunstall said.

"Thinking about riding over to Roswell, out to Chisum's South Springs Ranch," Pat said.

Billy watched as Pat finished his whiskey and stood, tall and thin, the shadow from his hat falling across his face accentuating his angular cheek bones.

"I need to talk to John about the situation around Sumner. The trouble between his men and the small ranchers. I got friends on both sides." Pat buttoned his wool coat over the gun and holster hanging on his narrow waist. Without moving he stared straight into the flames in the fireplace, his black eyes reflecting sadness. Saying nothing else he turned and walked out, his back straight.

Shortly two men, Frank Baker and Billy Morton, walked in and sat down at the bar. Glancing around, they spied Billy. They held their gaze but then turned their backs and ordered drinks. Tunstall shook his head when Billy started to stand.

"They're part of Dolan's gang," Billy said. "I might as well see if they're looking for trouble."

"Not here." After a moment Tunstall left, saying he had to turn in.

Billy settled down and scooted his chair so his back was to the bar. He drank his coffee, never looking in the direction of the two men again. After a while, Billy walked over to the fireplace and stared into the red embers. What was it about Pat that made Billy always consider who she really was, a woman, and who she wasn't, a man? The men's clothing did not change the way she felt inside when she took the time to feel her emotions. And yet just minutes earlier, she was eager to face two men, gun barrel to gun barrel. That was a part of her too but right now, as she looked into the flickering blue flames, it was not the most important. For at that instant she wished she could have looked into the eyes of Pat and told him who she really was, regardless of the consequences. The urge she had experienced to press her body against his and touch her lips to his had been especially strong. She would have liked to tell herself that that urge was because he seemed consumed with sorrow, unable to deal with the death of his wife. Except she would not lie to herself. She wanted Pat as any woman strongly wants a man. With the toe of her boot, she kicked a red coal that had popped out onto the blackened stone hearth. Billy walked slowly back to the hotel room without bothering to check the bar to see if the two men were still sitting there.

15

The next morning Billy stepped out of his Wortley Hotel room onto the wooden sidewalk along Main Street. It was a blue sky day with the sun a bright orange. Adjacent to the building was the Dolan store and across the street was the McSween home. After getting his horse from the hotel's stable, Billy rode along the main street to the sheriff's new building, a one-room office with a jail cell dug beneath it. He slowly dismounted and stood in the street looking into the small window at the two men inside. He opened the door and walked in.

"Hello, Brady," Billy said.

At a desk, George Peppin, deputy, and William Brady, sheriff, looked up from a poster they were studying. Both stood straight up, hands hanging by their holstered pistols.

"Wanted to let you know I was in town." Billy leaned back against the door frame, his arms crossed. "Or maybe you've heard."

"No problem there," Brady said.

"Thought me and you might talk some," Billy said not moving. "Yeah?"

Peppin stepped back from the desk, gaining more space.

"George," Brady said, "why don't you check out the Dolan store, have them deliver a bale of hay to our shed?"

Peppin frowned. "You want me to do that? Now?"

"Yeah George, I do."

Peppin grabbed his hat, shoved it onto his head. He walked past Billy closely, but not looking at him or bumping into his elbow.

"What's on your mind, Billy?" Brady sat down on the edge of the desk.

"That's what I was going to ask you."

"Okay. Heard you went to work for the Englishman."

"I did."

"That puts you at odds with your old bosses."

"And their hands."

"And their hands."

"How about you?" Billy continued to lean against the door frame, a smile on his face.

"I'm trying not to take sides. I'll do what the law requires."

"That's all I wanted to know. Their men don't bother me."

"We had your ex-buddy Evans in jail here for a while, but your new boss the Englishman vouched for him. Said his stolen horses had been returned. We let him go. Strange situation."

"Brady, you gave me a job when I first got here. I appreciate that. Now I'm not looking for trouble, certainly not from you." Billy walked over and stood in front of the sheriff. "Though if any of that Dolan bunch comes looking for me, there'll be a shooting. I don't back down."

Brady nodded, "I figured that."

"You might just pass that on. I'll be ready." His smile faded. "But I'll promise you this—I won't draw first. So don't come looking for me. I'll be around."

Billy walked out.

In the McSween-Tunstall mercantile store, Billy stood in front of Mrs. McSween.

"I'd heard you changed sides, went to work for Mr. Tunstall."

"That's right." Billy answered.

Mrs. McSween was wearing a dark blue dress with white trim. Her hair was gathered in the back in long curls, held in place by a wide white ribbon. As usual she was attractive and looked very business like, yet her smile seemed more than friendly, meant especially for Billy. "I'm pleased about that and I'm glad you stopped by. Is there anything I can do for you?"

"No, ma'am."

"No new shirts or neckerchiefs?"

"Not for now. I'm just taking it easy for several days in town before I head back to the ranch."

"Oh?"

"Playing cards in the evening and sleeping late."

"Well now, Mr. McSween has ridden into Mesilla to see the probate judge about a case involving a will, that of a man named Fritz who died." She frowned. "His relatives claim my husband kept the ten thousand dollars of life insurance. He didn't, not a single red cent."

"Some people don't have much trust in others."

"Mr. McSween can certainly be trusted. He never got the ten thousand. Anyway, he won't be back for several days." She moved slightly, one step closer, her eyes never looking away.

"I do like the fresh smell of your perfume, Mrs. McSween."

"Well, thank you. My husband always buys it for me when he goes to St. Louis." She placed her hand on Billy's arm. "I would like some company. Perhaps you'd like to stop by tonight around eight. I understand you like coffee."

Billy watched her unwavering gray eyes.

"It's nothing special," she said. "And I don't want to interfere with your card playing. However I would enjoy having a cup of coffee with you"

"I'd like that."

"Please come in the west door. The east side of the house belongs to Mrs. Elizabeth Shields, my sister. Mr. McSween gave it to her for a dollar when she and her husband came to town needing a place to live. Elizabeth is always writing in her diary or her memoirs, as she calls them."

Billy rubbed his chin with the palm of his hand but said nothing.

"But please come by, it'll just be the two of us."

"I'll be there. I always enjoy talking to you."

"Talking? Why yes, we can talk as long as you like." She squeezed Billy's arm. "And if we are going to spend some time together, we need to do it now. Around Christmas Mr. Chisum, Mr. McSween, and I are going to St. Louis to do some shopping."

16

Intent on keeping the promise to spend some quiet time with the McSween woman, Billy knocked softly on the door. The tapping was barely audible above the noise of the rushing water of the Rio Bonito River forty yards behind the house. A blowing cold west wind swept down from the Captain Mountains and Sierra Blanca.

"Come in. It's really cold out," Mrs. McSween said, swinging the door open. She took his hat and coat, hanging them on a coat rack. Wearing a burgundy colored dress with a full skirt and tight bodice, she looked especially attractive, with a touch of rouge on each cheek. Again Billy wondered how it would be to dress in that way.

She led Billy to a dining-sitting room with an oak table, chairs, and a red and silver upholstered divan. Billy, glancing around, sat down at one end of the divan. Susan sat down on the other, a glass of sherry in her hand. The room was well lit with lamps sitting on the two end tables. A crystal decanter of sherry, half-empty, was on the dining table, casting a red glow on the white tablecloth.

"When my husband is gone I like to drink a little sherry. Would you like a bit?"

"Coffee'll do."

"It's perking."

"I can smell it."

"I see you're still wearing your gun."

"Yes, ma'am. It's part of me."

"It looks so long and hard in that holster pushing against your leg, so uncomfortable. Why not take it off? Lay it on the table?"

Billy stood, undid the thin leather tie-down strip from around his leg, folded the belt and holster together and placed them on the table. Standing there for a minute without moving, he looked over at her and smiled. "It does feel strange."

When Billy sat down Mrs. McSween moved over closer. Taking his right hand, she placed hers against his, matching thumb against thumb.

"You have such small hands but with long slender fingers. Why my hand is wider."

Billy said nothing.

"But I'll bet they are very sensitive hands." She covered the top of his hand with her other.

"Maybe that's why you're very good with that gun. I hear you killed three Apaches in the blink of an eye." She pressed her hands firmly against his. "Yet the women you've gone with probably like the tender nature of your hands, I'd imagine."

Billy was not going to comment on either statement. These were topics that didn't belong in the conversation, because Mrs. McSween was the subject to discuss, the reason for the visit.

Billy leaned back, trying to relax without making any attempt to break up their holding hands. But he was bothered by her nearness and determined to get some space between them. Still, Billy wanted the conversation to continue to learn how she behaved around a man in a close quiet situation.

"Do you know what I'm thinking, Billy?"

"No, Mrs. McSween, I don't."

"I'm thinking that it's strange that sensitive hands that are so good at firing a gun accurately are also so good at touching a woman. That tenderness and killing are so close together in a man's hands."

She released his hand, picked up the sherry and drank it. She slowly refilled the glass and turned back to Billy.

Her hand covered his again as her thumb softly rubbed the top his knuckles, following the hard peaks and soft valleys.

"There is something else," she said. "You do have the coldest blue eyes. They give me chills when you look at me. That is unless you're smiling. Then your expression, the glint of those blue eyes, completely changes. When that happens, I get warm all over."

Billy smiled and she laughed.

"And for tonight you should call me Susan." She squeezed his hand.

Suddenly her smile faded. She stood, walked to the end of the table and stared out the window, her back to Billy. For sometime neither spoke.

"I guess you've heard the talk around town about me," she said.

"No. I only hang around with gamblers and the talk is certainly not about the ladies living here."

"Well, what do you talk about?"

"Hardly nothing at all."

"About the women that work in the bars?" She continued to look into the window at her reflection, the white face framed by the red hair looking especially dark in the lamplight.

"Yeah, we do that."

"About their performance? Which ones are the best? Is that what your talk covers?"

"Yes, Mrs. …Susan, we do talk that way."

"Do you yourself say which one pleases you the most?"

"Some times."

"My husband never talks about women." She turned to face him, picking up her sherry and sipping from the glass. Her hip pressed lightly against the oak table.

Billy said nothing, his eyes looking directly at hers.

"When you met Mr. McSween at the bank, did he say anything about, well…or talk to you strangely?"

"No, not at all."

"He is a fierce competitor, yet he is also a sweet and kind man. But there is one thing he has little interest in…procreation."

Billy shifted his leg letting one boot rest on the other, rubbed his chin with a forearm, and watched as she finished her sherry and poured another.

"I like drinking sherry. It makes me feel young again, almost giggly."

A swirling gust of wind rattled the front window causing Billy to quickly spin around to face the front door.

"It's just the wind," she said. "I need to set the coffee off the stove, let it cool down so the grounds will settle."

Moments later she was back, and turned the wick down on the lamp at the opposite end of the divan from Billy. She blew into the chimney of the lamp next to him, extinguishing it, and sat down close to Billy.

"People do talk about me around town, I know." She refilled her glass. "And they don't say pleasant things. It's statements about me and men. For that reason the ladies of the town don't associate with me. I have no friends. I do have secrets."

Billy sat without moving, saying nothing. He looked at Susan, her eyes a dark gray in the dim light.

"Consummation of our marriage was not easy." She placed her hand on Billy's thigh, a slight frown on her face, her eyes never leaving his.

Even through the thick woolen trousers Billy could feel the warmth of her hand.

Billy took a deep breath, yet did not glance away, while the wind continued to rattle the windows and doors.

"We were married in Atchison, a big place. You know he was a Presbyterian minister. Here life is more difficult. Lincoln is a very small town." Her thumb slowly caressed his thigh while her eyes remained focused on his. She set her glass on the table without looking away. Her lips formed a slight frown when he remained motionless.

Billy glanced down at Susan's hand, thinking that now, at this moment, she certainly deserved some sort of explanation. To say nothing didn't seem right. Was now the time to gamble, to tell the truth to someone who might or might not understand? Was now the time to find at least one person to confide in—a woman who would know the secret and respect the need for Billy to remain a woman who had secrets of her own?

"Susan, how long have you lived here?"

"Since March of '75."

"Late that year there was a shooting in Silver City, a deputy sheriff was killed."

When Susan remained silent Billy sat up straight, halving the space between their faces. He studied her expression. The frown was gone while the pressure of her hand was not.

"You heard nothing about a deputy sheriff being killed?"

"Maybe. I think I saw something in the paper, but I've forgotten." She leaned forward. "Why do you ask?"

"I just thought you might have heard something."

Her breasts touched Billy's arm.

"No one was ever caught."

Her breasts, warm through her velvet bodice, pressed against Billy. With his hip pushed against the end armrest, there was no more room to slide backward. "I lived there at the time, in Silver."

Her face was close to Billy's, her breath sweet from the sherry.

"Rumor has it that he was killed by a girl."

Her tongue touching her upper lip, she leaned firmly against Billy and, even with the cold wind, the room seemed especially warm.

"A girl that was really good with a gun."

Her lips parted as her eyes closed.

"She rode out of Silver and was never heard from or seen again."

Susan leaned back suddenly, her eyes wide open. "What are you talking about?"

Again, Billy rubbed his chin, aware of how smooth it was.

"What are you saying? What does this have to do with now?"

"Nothing. Nothing, really."

Her eyes crinkled at the corners as she leaned backward.

"It's just something I think about, having been there at the time, a girl killing a deputy."

"Did you know her?" Her voice was just above a whisper.

Billy looked away at the dim lamp on the small table at the end of the divan.

"Did you know her? Were you friends?"

"I knew her." Billy turned to face Susan.

"Well? Did you know her well?"

Suddenly an urgent knocking at the door.

Her hand quickly moved from Billy's thigh and Susan rose, opening the door.

"Why, Elizabeth, come in."

"The wind is blowing so hard, I thought you might… Oh, hello!"

"Elizabeth, meet Billy Bonney."

17

Memoir, page 21

Emil Fritz, a partner of Dolan and Riley during the time their mercantile store was in Fort Stanton, left the New Mexico Territory to visit family in Germany in 1874. He died shortly after arriving. In September of '76 McSween was appointed as the executor of the estate worth $10,000.00 dollars, the value of Fritz's insurance policy. McSween traveled to New York to collect the money for the relatives of Fritz, a brother and sister. Some said he had been paid by the insurance company when he was in New York, something he vigorously denied. He claimed he hadn't been paid and therefore could not pass the money on to the family.

On December 24,1877, John Chisum joined Alexander and Susan McSween in Anton Chico. Later that day the three arrived in Las Vegas, a few miles north of the small town. They intended to spend Christmas in Vegas before heading out for St. Louis in a large covered buggy, which they planned to fill with supplies for their store in Lincoln.

But in Mesilla, on December 27, 1887, the brother and sister of Emil Fritz, with the encouragement of Dolan, filed a complaint against McSween. The two claimed that McSween was holding the insurance money. Subsequently, a warrant was issued for the arrest of Alexander McSween by District Attorney Rynerson in Judge Bristol's court in Mesilla.

On Christmas day 1877, 170 miles south of Las Vegas, a blowing snowstorm was hitting Lincoln, plus all the farms and small ranches along the Rio Ruidoso and Rio Bonito. The storm moved east, sweeping across the flat land of the Pecos River Valley. It was the worst winter in a decade.

Billy sat at the table of Charley and Manuela Bowdre. They had just finished a dinner of turkey, dressing, canned green beans, and cornbread with pumpkin pie for dessert. Dick Brewer had eaten with them and had left saying he needed to get back to check on his stock, Christmas day or not.

A fired roared in the stone fireplace of the one-room cabin. Even though the cabin was warm and pleasant, the gusting wind rattled the cedar shingles, the window and door. A pine tree decorated with angels made from corn shucks and white ribbons stood in one corner. Another corner was occupied by a large butter churn. In the center of the room, a ladder led up to a loft for sleeping.

Manuela filled their cups with hot coffee poured from a pot that had been sitting on the stone hearth. She sat back down at the table.

"Dick is as handsome as ever with that curly blond hair and blue eyes," Manuela said.

"The women sure think so, " Charley added. "He's a good man whenever there's trouble. He needs to find a woman and settle down. Have a baby or two."

"We want to have kids," Manuela said to Billy.

"Yeah, we do," he answered. "To really enjoy Christmas, you need kids around."

"Josiah Scurlock, or Doc, has a home half a mile on up the Ruidoso," she said. "He was a dentist before coming out here. A number of years back he married my friend Antonia Herrera from San Patricio. Now they've got a passel of kids. We need our own."

Charley nodded. "We do. I grew up in Mississippi on a large farm. I had four sisters and five brothers. I like kids. And we are going to have some."

"I believe you met Doc and Antonia at the baile," Manuela said.

"I did," Billy said.

"Me and him work together farming, helping each other in the fields, taking out tree stumps and boulders." Charley said. "When the vegetables are ready we harvest them, assist each other, take a load of corn to Stanton. That is, when I can keep Doc sober and out of Lincoln."

Billy smiled. "Yeah, I heard, he's always getting in one scrape or another."

"There's some land for sale up above Scurlock's place," Charley said.

"We have six cows Charley milks," Manuela added, "and I use the cream to churn butter. We can sell all we make in Lincoln or Stanton, more if we had it."

"That land I was talking about, it would be a good place to start your own spread, mostly for cattle and maybe hay, since it's not very level. Regardless, we'd help." Charley gave Billy a straight look. "One thing, all the cows we have, each I bought, paid for with money from this farm."

"We didn't even take a maverick," Manuela said.

Billy nodded, understanding that Charley was telling him he was scrupulously honest.

"You should go check on that land," Charley said. "Like I said we'll help."

"Matter of fact Fred Waite and I are looking into starting a place." Billy rose. "I really should be getting back to Tunstall's ranch."

"It's a long ride," Manuela said as she and Charley stood side by side their arms around each other.

Billy slipped on a heavy canvas coat lined with wool and slapped a dark hat down hard on his head.

"That hat," Manuela said, "it looks so much like the one Charley wears."

"A little more beat up," Billy said.

The strong wind had started to swirl snowflakes against the window.

"Why not stay here for the night?" Charley asked.

"I got to get back, check on the cattle in this snow storm. Make sure they're not driven too far east. Waite's there, but I need to give him some help."

"I've got all our stock in the barn," Charley said.

"Gracias for the fine dinner, Manuela." Billy shook Charley's hand, gave Manuela a hug, and put his hand on the door latch, but turned to face the two. She now had one arm around Charley, holding him tightly. She rested her head on his shoulder.

"Feliz Navidad, Manuela, Charley," Billy said.

"Feliz Navidad, Billy," Manuela said.

"Next year you folks will have a baby to share Christmas day with. I'd bet on it." Billy stepped through the door pulling it shut tightly.

Two days after Christmas, outside of Las Vegas, the sheriff of San Miguel County with a posse of over twenty men overtook Chisum and the McSweens on their way to St. Louis. He arrested both men, roughly. Chisum was thrown to the ground and McSween was dragged away by several from the posse.

"He's not armed," Susan screamed leaning out the door of the buggy.

"Let him up," the sheriff said to the men holding the lawyer. "Mr. McSween, I got a telegram from Attorney General Catron claiming you got ten thousand dollars of insurance money belonging to the heirs of Emil Fritz."

"That's a lie," McSween said.

"A formal arrest warrant from Judge Bristol in Mesilla is on the way," the sheriff said. "Tie his hands."

Both men were taken back to Las Vegas where Chisum was released on bail and McSween was locked up. Susan rented a room in the downtown Plaza Hotel. The next day she visited her husband in jail. He made arrangements for a driver to take her back to Lincoln in the covered buggy.

A week later McSween was taken to Mesilla to face Judge Bristol who fixed bond at eight thousand. For several minutes the courtroom was quiet.

"Eight thousand seems high, Your Honor," McSween said.

"Mr. McSween, you are accused of embezzling ten thousand dollars, that you have that money someplace in a bank. I know you deny that. A trial will decide who's right."

"Your Honor, I can assure you I've never collected a single cent from the Merchants Life Insurance Company of New York. They are the ones that should be brought to trial."

"This proceeding is over. Bond is eight thousand."

In late January a Deputy Sheriff left Mesilla with orders to deliver McSween to Sheriff Brady in Lincoln. On the way McSween convinced the deputy that his life would be endangered if he were turned over to Brady. Exacting a promise from McSween not to leave town, the officer released his prisoner in Lincoln and returned to Las Vegas without stopping to notify Brady of his actions.

By February of 1878 both McSween and Chisum had posted bond in Judge Bristol's Court in Mesilla and had returned to the vicinity of Lincoln. Tunstall remained in town while Billy stayed at his ranch, keeping watch over the cattle along with Fred Waite. The Fritz case had not been resolved.

Baxter and James Dolan had ridden hard from Mesilla, covering 160 miles in five days. On February 12 they pulled their horses up in front of Brady's home located in Walnut Grove, a small canyon six miles east of Lincoln. The clear, cold Rio Bonito ran in the small valley, separating the hills on either side.

"I'll tell you one thing for sure," Dolan said as he dismounted, "when you meet Mrs. Brady, she'll be dressed as if heading to church."

"Yeah?"

"Anglo men, they marry a Spanish woman then treat her like a servant. Not my friend William. He's always buying her a new dress, jewelry."

A teenage boy followed by two younger ones came around the house and gathered the reins of their horses.

"William Junior, you've grown," Dolan said to the oldest.

"Yes, sir."

"Your dad around?" Dolan asked.

"He's there." William pointed to a large barn fifty yards north of the house.

At that moment a small door in the side of the building swung open and Sheriff Brady appeared. After shaking hands, the three men walked into the house and sat down in the kitchen. Brady's wife, Maria Chavez Brady, and three girls, eight to twelve, came into the room, the oldest holding a baby.

"My wife, daughters, and new son," Brady said.

Mrs. Brady took the baby. Then the twelve-year-old got mugs from the cabinets and poured coffee for the three men. Brady's family left the room.

"Nice big home here," Dolan said.

"With seven kids, I had to add on extra rooms."

For a while the three men sat silently drinking coffee.

"We've got a judgment of ten thousand dollars against McSween," Baxter said. "The Fritz case."

Brady sat with both hands around the mug and said nothing.

"We also have a Writ of Attachment," Baxter said, "from Judge Bristol for all of his personal property in both his store and home."

"That ought to put McSween out of business," Brady said, his eyes watching the other two.

"Yeah, probably," Baxter said. "I guess there's no problem with you doing your official duties. Attaching the property, assessing its worth."

"No, not if you have the Writ."

"We do," Baxter said, "except it's not the lawyer we want out of the way. He's just a nuisance."

"Meaning what?" Brady finished the coffee, setting the cup down.

"It's Tunstall we want."

"They are partners, but maybe not legally or officially," Brady said.

"The prosecuting attorney in Mesilla, Rynerson, thinks they're in cahoots," Baxter said.

"This leads us where, to do what?" Brady asked.

"The Writ of Attachment extends to the livestock on Tunstall's place."

"That's in the Writ?"

"That's the way we interpret it."

"A legal, official interpretation?"

"Brady, you remember how it was with the English in Ireland," Dolan said. "They didn't give a damn about legality or the laws of the land. They made their own, took our property."

"That's not here," Brady said.

"It's the same people. Tunstall wants all the land," Dolan said. "To have the only store in Lincoln, to monopolize trading, to control the cattle business with Fort Stanton and the reservation."

Brady stood up, walked to the back door and looked out.

"The English don't change," Dolan said.

"Whatever we do, I'd prefer that it be legal."

"You know, we know, Tunstall and McSween are partners. Rynerson agrees."

"Let's step outside," Dolan said.

The three men walked away from the house and stood in a small circle next to a barb wire fence.

"Brady, we've been friends for a long time," Dolan said, softly.

"Yeah."

"You're right this is not Ireland, but the Englishman is no different from the ones who took our property there."

Brady placed his boot on a strand of the barbwire fence, testing for tautness. "I am the law here. I try to do things legally."

"What we're talking about is legal," Baxter stepped in. "That's the way the Writ is interpreted. Get out to the Feliz. Inventory the cattle. Take the horses."

"Tunstall and his hands will fight," Brady said.

"So be it," Baxter said, stepping close to Brady and lowering his voice. "There needs to be gunplay. Tunstall has got to be eliminated."

Brady stared hard at the man standing in front of him.

"You don't have to go," Baxter explained. "You got a deputy. Get a posse together. Send them out there. Stay in town and keep watch on the McSween-Tunstall store. That way you're out of any repercussions."

"Brady, we've supported you up in Santa Fe. Dolan did too," Baxter said. "Worked to get you elected, took care of your scrip, helped to get this ranch."

"I still don't like it."

"Keep out of it. Stay in town," Baxter said. "Have your deputy, Mathews, lead the posse."

"If you need help, I'll get some of the men from my ranch. Baker, Morton and a few others," Dolan said. "But first you deputize some men from town to go out there with your deputy. Have a go at it. Then let me know if you need more men."

Brady looked at Dolan for seconds, his boot heel still hooked on the barbwire.

19

The group of men led by deputy Billy Mathews pulled up on a flat grassy area fifty yards from the Tunstall ranch house. In the posse were Andrew L. "Buckshot" Roberts and George Hindman.

"That's close enough," yelled Widenmann recently hired by McSween to work in the store or on Tunstall's ranch. He was standing on the porch, a Winchester cradled in one arm. On both sides of him men with rifles, including Billy, stood behind adobe bricks and sandbags stacked three feet high.

"We've got a Writ of Attachment for McSween's livestock here on the Feliz," Mathews hollered.

"McSween ain't got any horses or cattle here," the new man answered.

"That's not what we heard,"

"If you think you can come here and find out, try it!"

"You're interfering with the law," Mathews yelled. "You'll pay."

"Come on if you're so inclined."

The deputy huddled with his men for several minutes.

"We're not coming in now, but we'll be back," Mathews said.

Billy said nothing and gave Fred a smile. Clearly Mathews was not interested in going against the men with rifles, standing behind adobe bricks and sandbags. The threatening men wheeled their horses around and rode away.

Billy and Fred watched the posse disappear behind a rise into the ponderosa pines.

"They'll be back with more men next time," Billy said. "I'm going to ride into Lincoln, see what the boss wants to do."

"Billy, you think it's okay to go into Lincoln alone?" Fred said. "Brady and some more of his men along with the posse will be there."

"They won't face me, not on the street. Brady will keep things under control."

"Maybe I ought to go in with you," Fred said.

"No. You watch over things here. Besides with just one man going in, there's not going to be a shoot out."

"Well, I'm going," the new hand said.

In Lincoln, Widenmann talked with Tunstall and McSween. Billy remained silent. They decided to go back to the ranch and make a fight of it when the bigger posse returned. Tunstall said he would round up more men and meet at the ranch.

"If they want to fight, I'm ready. Let's get the ball started," Billy declared.

In Dolan's store, Mathews met with Brady and Dolan, while the rest of the posse milled around in the street, drinking the whiskey Dolan had given them.

"There's going be a shootout," Mathews explained, "and with all their men behind cover, it's not going to be easy."

"I don't like it, not out there on the Feliz," Brady said.

"Hell, I've got money in this store. It's time we settled this situation. Get rid of Tunstall," Mathews said.

"All we need is more men," Dolan said. "I'll send for Morton and Baker and some of the others."

Brady shook his head but said nothing else.

"We'll have the men from my camp and the posse gather on the Peñasco," Dolan said. "I'll go along. We can be there by the night of the seventeenth then head for the ranch at first light the next day."

On the evening of the seventeenth, Tunstall in his ranch house on the Feliz was informed by a friend, who had ridden in from Lincoln, that the posse was at a ranch on the upper Peñasco and would arrive the next day. The posse was now over forty men.

"That's too many for us," Tunstall said.

Billy sat cross-legged on the floor, cleaning his Winchester and two pistols.

"We'll take the horses, ride out to the open range and push them up a canyon," Tunstall said. "Let them inventory the cattle, which will consume the day. We'll just ride away."

"If we're going to fight them, here's the place," Billy said.

"I've changed my mind," Tunstall said. "I don't want to be responsible for men getting killed. That's not why I came here. We'll settle it in a court of law."

Fred Waite nodded in agreement.

"McCloskey, you have friends in the posse," Tunstall said. "In the morning you ride out, meet them. Tell them that this is no longer an armed camp. There will be no opposition when they come in to inventory the cattle."

Before daylight on February 18, Tunstall, Brewer, Widenmann, Middleton, and Billy pushed eleven horses across the open range north of the road leading to the Feliz. They stayed on the western edge of the Pecos Valley close to the mouths of the canyons. It was hilly country dotted with scrub oak on the slopes, ponderosa pine in the flats, and prickly pear, cholla, and mesquite trees in the arroyos. Due to the hills and vegetation, visibility was limited. Billy and Middleton lagged several hundred yards behind guarding the rear. By early evening Tunstall was herding the horses farther east where it was flatter with only the foot-tall grass to ride through for the trees had thinned out.

The posse reached Tunstall's ranch house to find the only man there was Gauss the cook. He met them on the porch unarmed, not smiling. McCloskey pointed out the tracks of the horse herd heading north on the open range. Mathews appointed and deputized Billy Morton to lead a smaller posse to ride after the horses, noting that the horses had to be inventoried too. Jesse Evans, Frank Baker, and one other man joined the group following the tracks.

20

An hour before sundown, Billy and Middleton were still riding several hundred yards behind Tunstall who was following a faint trail in the flat grassy area a quarter mile below. Brewer and Widenmann were ahead high on the hillside but below the trees and boulders on the rim of the hills.

Billy checked behind just as a group of riders came over a small rise. The two groups spotted each other at the same time. The posse spurred their horses heading for Billy and Middleton. The two split, Billy riding up to alert his friends on the hillside and Middleton riding down hard to warn Tunstall.

"Head up here," Middleton yelled to Tunstall sixty yards away.

Tunstall's attention was focused on the horses, trying to keep them in a small group.

Again Middleton with hands cupped around his mouth hollered at Tunstall who seemed not to hear. Further ahead, Billy reached the two on the hillside, motioning them to ride up towards the trees and boulders for cover.

The posse spotted Tunstall and a small group turned down toward him. He finally looked up, raised one arm in greetings, and started to ride toward the posse.

Middleton spurred his horse, jerked the reins to head him uphill toward Billy, and leaned over his saddle. When he reached the three he dismounted, joining them behind the rocks. They watched in the waning light as three men rode hard and fast toward Tunstall. The other dozen men continued on toward the four on the hillside but pulled up several hundred yards below them.

"We got to get down there," Billy said, his hand on the saddle horn, preparing to mount up. "Help Tunstall."

"We can't," Brewer said nodding at the group below them. "There's a dozen men between him and us."

"We've got to."

Brewer grabbed Billy's shoulder, holding it firmly in his big hand.

Further down the hillside the three men, Morton and two others, started firing their rifles. Tunstall slumped in the saddle. Another slug hit his head, killing him. He tumbled from the saddle.

"They've killed Tunstall," Billy said.

"Goddamn it, I tried to get him to follow me up here. He could have made it on that good horse of his," Middleton said.

"He didn't know what was going on," Billy said.

The part of the posse that had followed Billy continued to mill around several hundred yards below.

"They want no part of us up here," Brewer said.

"Tunstall's killed," Billy repeated.

The three men had ridden up to the body on the ground and sat on their horses looking down. The big group below huddled up before swerving their horses downhill riding toward the other three.

"It was Morton and two others from the Evans gang," Billy said.

"It was, no doubt about it," Brewer agreed.

"I'm going to kill those sonofabitches," Billy declared, "even if I get killed."

21

Billy, Brewer, Widenmann, Middleton, and Waite, who had joined them too late to become involved in the shooting action at the hillside, sat across from McSween in his home in Lincoln.

"Tunstall's dead," Billy repeated, staring McSween in the face.

McSween sat without moving, his right hand in a tight fist, his left, clasping it. Since the five had burst into his home with the news, he had said almost nothing, his eyes wide showing a lot of white.

"Damn it, we saw it. Know who did it," Billy said. "It's time to go after them."

"No," McSween said.

"No? What do you mean no? Tunstall was gunned down." Billy said. "Let's go."

"I need to think, get a plan," McSween said.

"The plan is to kill those bastards. The ones who murdered Tunstall. I'm going to do it, he was my friend."

"He was my friend too. But we need to do this legally," McSween said.

"You're right, Billy. It was murder," Brewer said. "And we need to get those who did it. But as McSween says, we need a plan, a legal one."

"A gunfight is not the answer," McSween insisted.

Billy stood, walked over to the window and stared out.

"There's officers of the law here," McSween said.

Billy turned, glaring at McSween, at his waist with no gun or gunbelt.

"I'll go by myself if no one else will," Billy said quietly and stepped toward the door.

"You know I'll go with you," Waite said.

"Hold it, you two," Brewer said. "We didn't say we wouldn't go. We just want to do it legally. Let's listen to Mr. McSween. Hear what he has to say."

McSween stood, glanced around the room, walked over to the fireplace and stared at the burning juniper logs for several minutes. Finally, as though talking to the hearth he said, "We can get no help from the sheriff, the district judge, or the district attorney. That's for sure."

"Wasting time." Billy shook his head at Waite, lips now in a hard straight line.

"So here's the plan to get the guilty ones." McSween turned to face the group. "And we can still do it legally. First thing in the morning, we go see John Wilson, Justice of the Peace. He has the power to deputize men if there has been a crime committed."

Brewer nodded while Billy stood at the window staring out.

"I'll spend all my time doing the legal work," McSween said. "I've sent Mrs. McSween back east. She'll stay there until this is over."

The following day in John Wilson's office, Brewer, Middleton, and Billy signed a statement that William Morton and others, some listed, others to be named, wounded and killed J.H. Tunstall. The town constable Atanacio Martinez attended the hearing and was given a warrant for the arrest of those involved in the murder. It listed the entire posse. Though willing to help, Martinez was hesitant. He organized a posse consisting of Billy, Brewer, Waite, Middleton, and fourteen others.

Storming into the Tunstall-McSween store, the posse arrested those men the sheriff had left there to watch the attached property.

When Brady rode into town he too was arrested but posted a two-hundred-dollar bond and walked away. At the Tunstall-McSween store, Brady arrested Fred Waite and Billy, who were clearing out Brady's men once again. The two were placed in the cellar jail.

Twenty or thirty men from both factions were still on the loose heavily armed and ready to start shooting. Alerted by several citizens from Lincoln, Captain Purington from Fort Stanton rode into town with infantry and cavalrymen. The Captain regarded the posse appointed by John Wilson as a mob and saw to the release of all the men they had jailed.

John Henry Tunstall was buried in a vacant lot east of his store on February 21. There were no mourners.

The day passed quietly though many citizens were involved in meetings to work at settling the feud between the two factions. Several men visited Brady, trying to convince him to call off the attachment of property in the McSween store. He refused. After the committee left, Brady unlocked the door to the jail where Billy and Waite sat on the one bunk.

"You're free to go," Brady said, "but I'm keeping your hardware."

"We'll meet again then we'll see." Billy's eyes bored into Brady.

The sheriff of Lincoln County said nothing.

"You're the law, the one who was in charge. You sent the drunk posse out to the Feliz. Told them to get Tunstall. You'll pay one day," Billy said.

The sheriff made no comment and turned away to step back into his office.

Standing next to the corral behind the Tunstall store, Billy looked at the freshly dug sod covering Tunstall's grave in the vacant lot. He turned to Waite.

"Fred, I'm going to get those bastards. Not today but soon. Give them the same chance they gave Tunstall."

Waite nodded.

"He was buried with no kinfolk. All alone, not a single goddamn flower," Billy said, his hands in tight fists. "He was a good and decent man, treated me like I was someone worthwhile. The only one to do that."

"He treated us good, that's for sure," Fred said as he untied the reins of his horse.

Billy pulled a 41 Colt from a saddlebag on his big gray, sliding it into his holster. The hell with wearing a dress like Mrs. McSween. The hell with learning how to face men as a woman. This was not the time to do that. What men understood was looking at the business end of a pistol. Billy mounted up and rode slowly down Main Street never glancing toward the Dolan-Murphy store.

22

The posse deputized by Justice of the Peace John Wilson called themselves the Regulators and considered that they were the rightful, legal group to enforce the law. The most active men were Dick Brewer, John Middleton, Fred Waite, Charley Bowdre, Frank and George Coe, Doc Scurlock and of course The Kid. Since the district attorney in Mesilla, Rynerson, had not approved the bond for McSween, the lawyer fled Lincoln. Brewer became the acknowledged leader of the Regulators. The number-one man on their arrest warrants signed by John Wilson was Billy Morton, who most believed had fired the fatal shots killing Tunstall.

The other faction, a posse controlled by Dolan but managed by Sheriff Brady, felt that they represented the legitimate law in Lincoln County. It seemed to all the other citizens that a shootout was inevitable.

Brewer received word that a group from the Dolan posse including Billy Morton was in a cow camp on the Rio Peñasco. On March 6 the Regulators, riding south from the Feliz, spotted five mounted men. Two broke off and raced northward through the foot-tall grass. It was Morton and Frank Baker. All the Regulators gave chase. For over an hour the pursuit continued with rifle fire punctuating the silence of the Pecos Valley. The horses of the two chased men finally gave out losing ground quickly to those behind. The two dismounted discarding their arms.

Billy was the first to reach them. Baker and Morton walked over, smiled, said hello and stuck out their hands.

"You sonofabitches, I don't know you. Don't come near me." Still on his horse, he pointed his Winchester at them and they backed away.

Brewer and the others rode up.

"We surrender to you, Brewer," Morton said. "If you promise us a safe ride back to Lincoln."

"As far as surrendering, you don't have a hell of a lot of choice," Brewer said sliding off his horse.

"We'll give you the same chance you gave Tunstall," Billy said, his rifle still pointing at the two.

"Hold it, Billy," Brewer said. "These are our captives. We'll take them back to Lincoln alive."

Billy eased the hammer down on his rifle. "Turn them over to Brady? That's going to do a lot of good."

"They go to Lincoln alive. Then we'll figure out something," Brewer said.

"I ain't making any promise," Billy said, shoving his rifle into its scabbard.

"Mount up," Brewer said. "We'll ride slow, give your horses a blow."

They headed up the Pecos toward Chisum's South Springs Ranch, Billy riding in the rear with Morton and Baker in the front. On the way they were joined by McCloskey, a man with friends in both the posse and the Regulators. He pulled in beside Brewer riding just behind the two prisoners. Brewer looked at him but said nothing.

Two days later, they reached Chisum's and put the prisoners in a room with a guard at the door. At noon the following day, the group left the ranch. They rode through Roswell before turning west on the main route to Lincoln. That night they camped next to the road.

After tying the hands of the two prisoners and looping a rope around the knots, they bound it to a juniper thirty yards from the camp.

The Kid, followed by Fred, bedded down two dozen yards away from the fire and opposite from the two tied men. Billy spent thirty minutes cleaning his rifle and pistol.

"We got a good view of those bastards if they try anything," Billy said leaning back on his saddle. He sat that way for a while before pulling a blanket and canvas sheet up around his neck.

Just before daylight McCloskey woke the two men, untied their hands, and handed them their Winchesters.

"They're loaded," McCloskey said. "But I got no extra shells. Your horses are saddled. Get the hell off the main road, head up the Blackwater Creek into the Capitan Mountains."

As they walked toward the horses, McCloskey stopped. "Only reason I'm doing this, you'd never make it to Lincoln alive."

The two led their horses away from the camp a hundred yards before mounting. They rode slowly in the deep grass with almost no sound.

In camp Billy poked Fred in the shoulder with his finger. "McCloskey let Baker and Morton go. I'm going after them."

'Two against one, I'm going."

"No, I can handle it. You stay and tell Brewer what happened."

The sun was just above the horizon when the fugitives noticed Billy on the big gray coming up behind them, a hundred yards in the rear. Both pulled on the reins, jerked their rifles from the scabbards, spun around in their saddles, and fired but missed. They spurred their horses, holding the Winchesters with one hand. The chase continued for thirty minutes with Billy gaining steadily. The two turned to fire often until their shells were expended. When Billy was twenty yards behind they pulled up, dismounted and pitched their rifles on the ground.

"Okay you bastards, now it's my turn." Billy slid off his horse.

The two looked at him but said nothing.

"Back up," Billy said not wanting to get too close, especially to Baker who was big and built like an ox. After they had stepped away, he reached down and picked up the two rifles. From his saddlebag he pulled out a box of forty-four caliber shells and removed two. He put one in the firing chamber of each gun then uncocked both before leaning them against two small cedars five yards apart.

"Now, you two can go for them."

"You'll shoot us down like dogs when we take the first step," Baker said.

"I should but I won't. I won't draw till you get your hands on the rifles." He pulled his pistol, flipped the loading gate, and extracted three shells. "That leaves me two, so we're even."

The two men stood without moving, looking at the rifles ten yards away.

"The others will be here shortly. Boys, we need to get the ball started, or I start shooting where you stand." He shoved his pistol into its holster.

Morton, a wiry young man, made the break first, racing quickly to the nearest Winchester. Baker was just behind but slower.

Morton grabbed the rifle and started to swing it toward Billy when the forty-one slug caught him in the right temple. His head was slammed to the side and he crumpled.

Billy dropped his pistol into the holster.

Baker at the second rifle grasped the barrel of the gun with one hand and shoved the forefinger of the other into the trigger guard, all the while swinging the gun around. Billy's bullet smashed into his head, just in front of his right ear. The rifle continued the swing until it pointed at Billy, who stood without moving. Baker's chest was heaving in and out, his thumb on the hammer finally cocking it, making a barely audible but ominous crack in the early morning silence. Slowly, ever so slowly, the rifle barrel began to inch downward. Baker's glassy eyes stayed glued on Billy while blood ran from his nose. The rifle fired, a loud ringing blast, the bullet kicking up dirt at Billy's feet. Baker's legs collapsed and he fell to his knees leaning forward propped up by the rifle, its barrel end pushed into the ground, his eyes still fastened on Billy. One arm fell to his side. The other remained stretched out, his hand grasping the rifle by its butt end. For a moment he remained motionless then fell face forward, his arm out straight, with his hand clutching the wooden stock of the rifle.

"Two down and a half dozen to go," Billy said. Slowly he reloaded five cartridges into his pistol before he slid it into his holster. He walked over to look at the two on the ground. Hearing the sound of distant running horses, Billy glanced down the narrow valley to see the group of Regulators riding toward him. Shortly they pulled up their horses and dismounted.

Brewer stood over the two dead men and studied their hands clutching rifles. "Run out of ammo?" he asked.

"Each had a cartridge," Billy said.

"Well, you killed them, armed, trying to escape," Bowdre said.

"Yeah."

"McCloskey's dead too," Brewer said. "We had an argument over cutting Baker and Morton loose."

"What are we going to do with these two?" Fred asked. "Can't just leave them."

Brewer removed his hat, wiped the sweat from his forehead and ran his hand through his thick curly blond hair. "Yeah, we need to do something."

"I saw a couple sheepherders about half hour ago as we passed by," Fred said. "How about I ride back, give them a buck. They'll bury them."

"Good enough," Brewer said.

"I heard him talk," Billy said, turning Morton over. "He's got a sister someplace out here. But no telling where. Yeah, we need to get them buried."

Billy looked at Fred and Brewer. "They did okay. Died good, guns in their hands."

23

Governor Axtell, with the encouragement of United States Attorney General Thomas B. Catron, traveled to Lincoln to investigate the situation there. It seems that Catron, who had a mortgage on the Dolan store and all its property, wanted Sheriff Brady designated as the law in the entire area around Lincoln, and the arrest warrant on McSween executed.

McSween, who had been hiding out in a line shack on Chisum's South Springs ranch, rode into Lincoln to have a conference with Sheriff Brady on March 9. His goal was to work out a compromise that would keep him out of jail until District Court opened and the conflict over the Fritz estate could be settled legally. It was his firm belief that if he went to jail his life would be worthless.

McSween was visited at his home by a friend with bad news. Governor Axtell had visited Lincoln that day. In a formal document the governor had declared that Justice of the Peace Wilson was illegally occupying that office. And that any appointments he had made were null and void. With this proclamation the Regulators could no longer claim to represent the law. Hearing the disturbing news, McSween again left town, heading to Chisum's ranch, unwilling to face Sheriff Brady, who still had the warrant for his arrest signed by Judge Bristol of Mesilla.

Several weeks after the visit of the Governor, Sheriff Brady visited the Chisum Ranch. The only person he met with was Susan McSween who had returned from Atchison two days earlier. They sat facing each other in a large room with a fireplace, bear rugs, several couches, and chairs with cowhide cushions.

"To get to the point, Mrs. McSween, let me say I have no intention of arresting your husband now," Brady said.

"You're carrying a warrant for his arrest."

"Yes, but in my judgment Mr. McSween will not fail to show up for the opening of District Court."

"He certainly plans to be there."

"I would like to talk to him," Brady said.

"He's not here."

Brady smiled. "I didn't think so."

"When I see Mr. McSween, if I do, I'll tell him you said he won't be arrested."

"It was good talking to you, Mrs. McSween." Brady stood.

"Likewise, Sheriff Brady." She also rose and walked him to the door.

He stepped out, turned to face her, but said nothing else before he mounted up.

That evening, several hours after dark, Billy rode up to the Chisum house. He dismounted and tied the reins to an iron ring on a cedar post.

"Hello, Billy," Mrs. McSween said, sitting in a rocker under the wide long overhang of the front porch.

"I thought that was you in the shadows," Billy said.

"And how are you tonight?"

"Been visiting Charley and Manuela Bowdre."

"That's a long ride."

"Yeah."

"Sheriff Brady visited me today," Susan said.

"Oh?"

"He says he's not going to arrest Mr. McSween, that he will see him when the District Court convenes."

"Do you believe him?"

"No."

"He got Tunstall killed," Billy said.

"They are going to kill my husband too, the first chance they get," Susan said. "Sheriff Brady will see to that."

"Not unless they arrest him before the court date. But we'll cover him going there."

"I've told Alexander a number of times we should go to St. Louis. And all the men don't carry guns. Alexander doesn't even do that here. We can make a living there."

Billy nodded and walked over to stand directly in front of her.

"Do you want to leave?" Billy asked.

"If it would save my husband's life."

The two remained motionless for sometime, neither talking until Billy finally turned to face the yard. The wispy shadows of the small mesquite trees shimmered in the slight breeze on the hard-packed dirt.

"What did you and Charley talk about? Shooting people?"

Billy didn't respond nor glance toward her.

"Is that all you men around this country know, shooting and killing?"

Now he spun to face her. "Mrs. McSween, it's the way things are here. It's life."

"Shooting and killing. There's got to be another way."

"It's what we have to do."

"You're good at it. I think you enjoy it." She stood and walked past Billy to the railing, but turned to face him. "You're no better than Dolan and his gang. The ones that murdered Tunstall."

Billy moved over and leaned against the railing, standing close to Susan, both still in the shadows. Her eyes flashed with the reflected moonlight.

"Is that what you believe?" he asked.

She breathed deeply, exhaling slowly, but never looked away.

"Is that what you believe?" he repeated.

"No, Billy, it's not." She placed her hand on his.

Billy stood there, saying nothing.

"I'm sorry I said that." Susan leaned forward briefly touching her lips to Billy's.

He sat down on the railing, leaned against the end post holding up the overhang and stared toward the dark horizon below the stars.

"It's okay," Billy said, thinking about what still had to be done. And he was the one that would have to do it. Maybe Susan was right, Billy was just like the others when it came to killing.

24

April 1, 1878 was a crisp sunny day. To the southwest, Sierra Blanca's snow-covered peak was stark white against a blue sky. Sheriff Brady, along with his deputies Billy Mathews (who had ridden with the posse that gunned down Tunstall) and George Hindman—plus another two—left the Lincoln County Courthouse. They walked along Main Street toward the Dolan store. The five men were spread out in case there was trouble, though none was expected. The street was deserted.

Billy, Fred Waite, and four others were crouched behind an adobe wall that formed a corral around the back of the Tunstall-McSween store. They had been there since before daylight.

"They're still two blocks up the street," Billy said, a Winchester in one hand.

"We ought to move out into the street," Fred whispered. "Meet them head on."

"No," Billy said.

"I don't like to hide and shoot," Fred said.

"We give them the same chance they gave Tunstall," Billy said quietly, his hat off, forehead barely above the top of the wall. His eyes were focused on the men walking toward them.

"Kid, I'm standing up before I start shooting," Fred said.

Billy glanced at him quickly then back at the men in the street.

"That's the way I'm going to do it," Fred emphasized.

"Okay," Billy agreed. "We stand then shoot."

Fred nodded.

"I'll stand first when they're about thirty yards," Billy said. "Nobody moves till I raise up."

The sheriff and his deputies, with Brady in the middle of the street, continued moving toward the Dolan Store. They were now fifty paces from the adobe wall back of the Tunstall store. The men on the wings checked the space between each building and behind the old, big cottonwoods on each side of the street as they went by. Brady faced straight ahead without shifting his eyes from side to side. In the center of town there were no horses at the hitching rails. Farther along the street to the east, several horses were tied up in front of the Wortley Hotel.

Billy stood saying nothing. He pointed his rifle at Brady and fired from the hip. The forty-four slug slammed into the Sheriff staggering him. The loud single shot reverberated between the buildings. Two others stood and fired a second later also hitting Brady. Gunfire raked the street. Hindman went down. On the south side of the street, the three deputies darted behind a building without being hit.

Billy jumped the wall and ran to the downed Brady, where he grabbed a new rifle and checked the sheriff's shirt pockets for warrants. Mathews fired from a window of the house he had entered through a side door. The bullet barely creased the flesh of Billy's upper leg causing him to spin and run to the adobe wall, vaulting over.

Lincoln became a silent town after the quick gun battle ended. Billy and friends stayed out of sight and the deputies did not go looking for them. An hour later, The Kid and the other shooters rode slowly out of town. Only when they were almost past gun range did the deputies venture into the street to fire at them.

The McSweens and Chisum came into town in the rancher's carriage when the shooting was over and quickly went to a friend's home. The body of Brady was still crumpled in the center of the street. Hindman lay on his back near the street's edge.

Mathews took charge and sent for help from a Captain at Fort Stanton. That afternoon the officer rode into Lincoln and assisted Deputy Mathews in arresting Alexander McSween. The Captain, fearing that McSween would be killed if he were put in the Lincoln jail, agreed to hold him at Fort Stanton until District Court convened on April 8.

The bodies of Brady and Hindeman were taken to the courthouse. With that accomplished, a close friend of the sheriff, along with the friend's wife, rode in a buckboard out to Brady's farm. The friend told his wife that it was going to be hard telling Mrs. Brady. He explained that her first husband and son were killed by Apaches back in the '60s.

At the farm, in the silence of the large dining room, the friend informed Maria Brady of her husband's death. She was surrounded by her seven children, the sixteen-month-old baby in the arms of the oldest girl. William Junior, his arm around his mother, led her to a chair. The younger children began to cry. Maria Brady was advised to stay at the farm until the next day when the burials of the two slain officers would take place.

After Catholic services the following day, the two men were buried in the Lincoln cemetery. With the coffin lowered, the Brady family walked slowly away surrounded by their friends. Mrs. Brady in black, with a black veil, was silent. She was held tightly by William. Clearly Maria Brady was expecting another baby. On that quiet morning, one of Brady's sons could be heard saying over and over, "They killed my daddy. They killed my daddy."

25

Andrew Roberts had an unknown past. Some said he had been a Texas Ranger although others said he was a fugitive from the Rangers. In 1878 he ran a small spread on the upper Ruidoso. He rode with the posse that went to the Tunstall ranch, although he was not with the small subposse that actually killed the Englishman. He was aware that the Regulators had a warrant for his arrest as a participant even though Governor Axtell had invalidated the warrants issued by Justice of the Peace Wilson. Roberts knew that Dick Brewer considered them valid, searching for anyone whose name was on the list. He figured it was time for him to clear out and sold his land to someone in Santa Fe.

Roberts was often called Buckshot because he had been hit in his right shoulder with a load of buckshot years ago. On April 4 Buckshot went to the post office of the small community of South Fork to wait for the mail and the check from Santa Fe paying him for his land. Nearby, on the Rio Tularosa, was a timber mill and a two-story house owned by Joseph Blazer, a friend of Buckshot's. The Indian Agent for the Mescalero Reservation rented the house for his family. His wife operated a restaurant in the large home.

Blazer received word from several Mescalero Apaches that a posse of mounted men was on the way to the mill. He immediately found Roberts.

"That group," Blazer told him, "can only be the Regulators. You need to clear out. I don't want a gunfight here with the women and children around."

After unhitching the packhorse that he had loaded earlier, Roberts mounted his saddled mule and took a faint, seldom-used trail leading away from the main road that the Regulators would ride in on.

Brewer, Billy, and the others arrived at the mill and placed their horses in a corral with high adobe brick sides. In the restaurant they ordered a late breakfast. Roberts, a mile away, watched as the postman rode along the main trail. He turned around and guided his mule to a hill overlooking the mill. Seeing no horses, he figured the Regulators had left. Riding slowly, studying the layout, he made it into South Fork and dismounted. He headed for the post office to see if his check had arrived.

When the men eating saw Roberts walking on the street, Charley Bowdre and George Coe walked out to arrest him. Bowdre pulled his pistol and Roberts raised his rifle to his hip. Both fired. Bowdre's slug hit Roberts in the midsection. The rifle slug hit Bowdre's gun belt, cutting it loose then ricocheted into Coe's gun hand. The battle was on.

The fatally wounded Roberts continued to fire from the hip, which was as high as he could lift the rifle due to the buckshot lodged in his shoulder. He made it into Blazer's office just as he ran out of ammunition. His last bullet had ripped into the right lung of Middleton, putting him out of the fight. Inside, he found Blazer's single-shot Springfield 45-60 and ammunition. Throwing a folded rug in the doorway, he lay flat and continued to shoot at his assailants. In front of the building all the brush and trees had been cleared, so he had a clear field of fire.

Dick Brewer, seeing the situation, ran below the crest of the hill and crawled behind a stack of logs a hundred yards down the slope. From here he could clearly see into the room where Roberts was holed up. Brewer fired once, his bullet slamming into the wall behind the cornered man. Roberts saw the smoke from the shot and aimed at the top of the logs.

Brewer raised his head to take another shot. Robert's thumb-sized forty-five slug hit him square in the forehead taking off most of his scalp. Brewer's head dropped. He never moved again. The golden curls were gone.

Billy, realizing Roberts was using a single-shot, wanted to rush the doorway when he saw that Brewer was dead. But the others talked him out of it. Bowdre said he'd shot Roberts dead center, dusting both sides, so the bullet had gone completely through. The man would not live through the night. There was no need to get more men shot. All the others agreed and the Regulators rode away, Billy the last to leave.

Roberts died the next day. He and Brewer were buried side by side, on the slope of the hill beneath the ponderosa pines.

"Oh, no," Manuela said, "not Dick."

"Yeah, he's killed," Billy said, sitting across from Manuela at the table in the Bowdres' cabin, with Charley at the window, staring out.

"Not Dick," she repeated. "He was always in the center of everything, the bailes, building a barn for a family, taking care of a torn-down fence for a friend. We all loved him."

Billy turned to face the fireplace, away from the pain in Manuela's face.

When the tears started to run down her cheeks, Charley sat down and put his arm around her shoulders. He handed over his handkerchief.

"I'm sorry," Billy said.

"No more golden curls," she said.

Billy stood. "I got to be going, talk to McSween."

Charley stared down at the table top, saying nothing.

Billy opened the door and stepped out, glancing back into the cabin where Charley sat close to his wife with his arm around her. She cried softly. Billy gently closed the door and walked over to his horse. He stood there momentarily before sliding a boot into the stirrup. So Brewer was dead.

A man and a woman, clearly in love. Caring for each other, feeling the sadness of losing a friend, but feeling it together. How would that be? Billy didn't know but was well aware that something was missing in her life. How to capture that sometimes vague, other times acute missing something she didn't know. But thoughts of Garrett and images of the lanky, dark-eyed man swung through her head. Billy eased up into the saddle and for several minutes held up on the reins. She looked at the small cabin with smoke drifting straight up from the chimney but disappearing quickly against the cloudy sky.

26

Memoir, page 36

On April 8 the District Court began in Lincoln. The proceedings did not go Dolan's way. Judge Bristol appointed John Copeland, not a Dolan man, to fill the vacant position created by the death of Sheriff Brady. Judge Bristol presided over the grand jury, men selected from the area, investigating the murders in Lincoln County. For the Tunstall killing, Jesse Evans, who had not been with the posse, and three of his gang were indicted. Dolan was listed as an accomplice. The Kid, John Middleton, and another were indicted for Brady's murder, with Fred Waite being indicted for the death of Hindman. For the killing at Blazer's Mill, Charley Bowdre was charged. Finally the grand jury fully exonerated McSween for embezzlement, even though Judge Bristol had encouraged the jurors to find the lawyer guilty.

Billy, Susan, and Alexander sat in the front room of the McSween home. Small split pieces of juniper burned in the stone fireplace. With the warrant on embezzlement voided, the couple had reoccupied their house. Other Regulators were in the kitchen discussing who should be their next captain.

Hearing a knock at the door, McSween opened it. The recently appointed Sheriff Copeland stood there.

"Come in," McSween said.

Inside, the Sheriff removed his hat, cleared his throat several times, and nodded at Mrs. McSween.

Billy inched to the edge of his chair, clearing his pistol handle.

"Kid," the Sheriff said, his eyes focused on Billy, "I'm not here to make a problem for you."

The sound of talking from the other rooms stopped.

"Have a seat," McSween said.

"Things need to settle down before anyone does anything." The Sheriff tugged on the lobe of his large misshapen ear.

"What are your plans?" McSween asked.

"I got a bucket full of arrest warrants." He shoved his hands into the pockets of his large wool coat, clearly away from his pistol covered by the long coat.

"And?" McSween asked.

"I don't plan to execute any, not now, not for a while. Let people alone, that's what I mean to do."

Billy remained on the edge of his chair but moved his hands away from his strapped-down pistol.

"The reason I stopped by, to let you know." Placing his hat back on his head he turned to leave.

"That's appreciated, the right thing to do," McSween said. "Stay awhile. Eat dinner with us."

"Thanks, but I got to talk to others." The sheriff stepped out and closed the door softly.

For several minutes no one said a word. The buzz of conversation started in the kitchen again.

"Tunstall, Brady, Brewer, all dead, shot, killed," Susan said. "Alex, it's time for us to leave. You could be next."

"Not now. I'm sorry about Tunstall and Brewer, but things are starting to go our way."

"Now that you are in the clear, no warrants out for your arrest, we could leave with no legal problems."

"No, Susan. The Dolan store is about to go bankrupt. Our livelihood is here." He rose and, taking the poker, pushed several logs closer together, causing the burning juniper to pop.

Billy watched the two of them argue, neither angry, but clearly Susan was frightened about their future in Lincoln.

"Just because the Sheriff's not going to arrest anyone now, that won't stop the violence," Susan said. "There's still anger and a desire for revenge on both sides."

"We're not leaving," McSween said.

"Please, Alexander."

"I'm not running. We're staying."

Susan rose, hands on hips, and faced her husband. She shook her head slowly.

"Staying in this house. And running our store and bank," McSween emphasized quietly.

"There will be more killings." She quickly turned and walked out of the room.

"What do you think, Billy?" McSween asked.

"Susan's right, the shootings will go on. Maybe you ought to listen to your wife."

McSween stood for a while facing Billy, but said nothing. He left to join the other men in the kitchen. Billy buttoned up and stepped outside. Unhitching his horse, he mounted and rode slowly out of town, headed for San Patricio.

27

For several weeks neither the posse, loyal to Dolan, nor the Regulators, supporting McSween, met. Both sides laid low. Billy went to several bailes in San Patricio, but with Brewer dead there was a somber atmosphere. He rode out to the Tunstall ranch, talked to Gauss, ate the meals the cook fixed, and checked on the livestock.

When on the range, Billy stopped, dismounted on the side of a hill out of the spring winds, and sat on a log. She studied the small Feliz Valley, the dark line of trees lining the river. From the runoff of melted snow, the stream was white and foaming in many places, churning against the rocks, but deep and cold in narrow stretches. Several times she grabbed the oily rag from the saddlebag and cleaned her pistol and the new Winchester taken from Brady. But mostly, she looked out over the rolling sea of grass along the river. Her thoughts drifted back to the time she first rode into Arizona Territory, using the name Billy Bonney. All the passing days, every event that had transpired, each shooting she had been involved in, all of that made it harder to return to the woman she was. That was becoming clearer the longer she remained Billy. And she was a woman, no longer a girl, which was also becoming clearer whenever she stopped to think about it. With all the action that had occurred recently, she hadn't had much time to mull over who she was. But when she did it seemed the thoughts of being a woman were more intense. She stood, snapped the brim of her hat down hard and mounted up. The big gray always felt good between her legs, giving her a sense of power. Still in some ways it made her more sensitive to her needs as a woman. She turned into the wind and rode slowly across the valley

On April 29, 1878, a large posse rode out of Lincoln. It was composed of the men who were sworn in by Brady before his death, and of newly recruited cowboys from the Seven Rivers area, men who disliked Chisum, and hence McSween for siding with the cattle king of the Pecos. They stopped at the Fritz ranch ten miles east of town.

On their way to the Coe spread, Frank Coe and two friends rode past the Fritz ranch. They were fired upon. The two friends were killed and Coe was captured, but he was released shortly. The posse then rode to the outskirts of Lincoln. The following morning they started shooting at the Regulators, who had been hanging around town. Although an extensive gun battle ensued, no one was seriously wounded.

That afternoon, heeding the request of a confused Sheriff Copeland, a lieutenant from Fort Stanton rode into Lincoln with a squad of Black cavalrymen, the Buffalo Soldiers. With the help of these men, the Sheriff arrested thirty or so combatants from both sides. On May 4, not knowing what to do with such a large group, the Sheriff released all, telling them to go home and quit fighting.

For several weeks, the situation remained peaceful, but Dolan was at work in Santa Fe talking to a man, Attorney General Thomas B. Catron, who led the Santa Fe Ring. On May 28 Governor Axtell replaced Sheriff Copeland with George Peppin, who sided with Dolan. Peppin had new warrants for the arrest of the Regulators, federal warrants because the fight at Blazer's Mill had occurred on government land. Weeks later, Judge Bristol of Mesilla indicted Billy and the others for the murder of Roberts when they failed to show up in court on the required June 22 date. Billy was now wanted by the territory for the murder of Brady and by the United States for the murder of Roberts.

Enjoying the warm summer day, Billy rode into the Coe ranch while the court session in Mcsilla was still going on. Billy pulled up at the hitching rail where a new man stood. He was tall and gangly with red hair and white teeth displayed by a wide smile. Billy, who had been riding for almost eight hours, slid from his horse and gave a tired look to the young man.

"You must be Billy Bonney," the man said, stroking the big gray. "I heard a lot about you from the Coes when they hired me."

Billy nodded.

"I'm Tom O'Folliard from Texas."

Billy pulled off his glove and shook hands.

"Heard about The Kid, down in Texas, the way you can shoot, with the Winchester and Colt. Wanted to meet you."

"Yeah?"

"I'll take your horse back to the barn, feed him some corn."

Billy handed him the reins.

"I want to join up, get in the fight." The young man had no smile on his face now, his lips a long straight line.

"Can you shoot?"

Tom glanced away then back at Billy. "Yeah, some."

"Some won't do it."

"I'll learn."

"Tom, after you take care of my horse, get Frank's buffalo gun and a box of cartridges. I'll teach you how to shoot. If you can handle that cannon, you can shoot anything."

For almost a week, several hours each day, Billy worked with the new hand. After practice, the two sat on a hillside wiping their guns with oily rags.

"Always clean the guns, always," Billy said. He looked at Tom, at the mop of reddish-brown hair, the light brown eyes with golden flakes. Though not handsome, he was attractive. "Where you from in Texas?"

"Around Uvalde in South Texas on the Nueces, in the brush country. It's south of the trail from San Antonio to El Paso."

"You got family there?"

"Aunts and uncles. A Grandmother, Mrs. Mary Jane Cook. She raised me. Ma and Pa died when we were in Mexico. Smallpox. My uncle come got me."

"What are you doing out here?"

"I came because I wanted to see a lot of the country before I die. And like I said, I heard stories about you."

"Down there in Uvalde, you ever hear of Silver City over there on the western edge of New Mexico Territory?"

"I have now, but not when I was in Texas."

Billy stopped wiping his gun and looked away.

"How come you asked?" Tom wanted to know.

"Just curious, that's all, just curious. Maybe that would be the place to go one day," Billy said.

"Most of the land is taken. No free range like here."

Billy nodded and folded his cleaning rag, placing it in a leather pouch. "Tom, when you give it your attention, you can shoot. We've practiced enough."

Tom slid his pistol into his holster, snapping the leather holding loop over the hammer of the forty-five.

"Just remember what I said. When you get ready to shoot a pistol, concentrate on the target. The gun will aim itself. And you be damn sure you get in the first shot. One that counts."

Billy and Tom walked back to the ranch house. Tom was smiling. Billy was silent, thinking about things to come. Other thoughts came to Billy too, like how much longer the fight should, and would, go on.

A day later, with his recent recruit and other McSween supporters, Billy retired to San Patricio. With Tom tagging along, Billy found the absence of Dick not quite so intense. After a big dinner at Dow's store, the group slept in an abandoned, one-room adobe cabin.

The following morning several Mexican men, local residents, rode up to the house and told Billy that a large group of men was a mile away to the north. They were on the road coming into town and riding hard. The McSween group mounted up, heading eastward. They were out of sight in the pines and juniper trees by the time Peppin and his large posse arrived. Shortly after dark they were at Chisum's South Fork ranch.

On the Fourth of July the posse showed up at the ranch and a long range fight ensued. It lasted half a day with few casualties. Evidently the Sheriff had no intention of storming the well-fortified ranch house, because he gathered his men in the middle of the afternoon and rode away.

28

Memoir, p 44

On July 15, 1878 the deciding battle between the Peppin posse backing Dolan and the Regulators supporting McSween started. The fight raged in the middle of Lincoln. Both sides fought to dominate the mercantile business of southeastern New Mexico. This included the federal contracts to supply beef, corn and other provisions to the military at nearby Fort Stanton and to the Mescalero Apache Indian reservation.

On the night of July 14, the Regulators slipped into town. They occupied the McSween home, the Tunstall mercantile store and two buildings further west, all on the north side of Main Street.

The following morning, during a dust storm, the posse rode into town and occupied the Wortley Hotel on the east end of town and the torreon on the west end. From the hotel, they immediately started shooting at the McSween residence. Billy and others raced to the McSween home and returned fire. The war was on.

For four days it was a standoff, then someone shot the horse of a cavalry messenger. The military could not accept this and do nothing. Midmorning, on the nineteenth, Colonel Dudley, from Fort Stanton, other officers, and troopers with a cannon, rode into Lincoln, setting up on the west end of town. Although the colonel claimed to be impartial in the fight, he immediately pointed his cannons at the nearby buildings occupied by men of the McSween faction. *The buildings were quickly evacuated. Numerous men crossed the river and left, others made it to the McSween home.*

That afternoon Susan McSween, ignoring all the rifles pointed at her, walked down Main Street to confront the Colonel, imploring him to stop the battle for the sake of the women and children in her home. She was ignored and returned to her home. Later that evening, she and her sister Elizabeth Shields and the children fled to the Tunstall store which was no longer being fired upon. A few hours later the McSween house was set on fire, forcing the men to flee to the safety of the river and trees. Some were killed in their escape attempt.

McSween and his supporters, almost thirty strong, rode into Lincoln on the night of July 14 from Chisum's ranch. Sheriff Peppin, Dolan and several of the posse were at the Wortley Hotel. Four others from the posse were at the torreon, a fifteen-foot-high, round rock building with shooting ports. It had been constructed years earlier to protect the town from Indian raids. Many of the men in the posse were out searching the countryside for the Regulators. The men supporting Dolan, including Sheriff Peppin, made no hostile moves against the McSween men who were splitting up, some going to the Tunstall store, others to the McSween home, and a dozen went to two buildings on the west end of town.

Alexander joined Susan in the living room of their large U-shaped adobe building. Half dozen Regulators had gone into the kitchen for coffee. In the east wing of the house were Susan's sister, Elizabeth Shield, and her five children. Elizabeth's husband was in Las Vegas.

"I'm through running," McSween said. "Sleeping on the ground like a hunted coyote. I've had enough. This is my home, and it's where I'm staying. We've got to settle all of the legal problems in court."

"Let's leave and go to St. Louis."

"No. They are not going to chase me out of town," McSween said. "This is our home."

"No, it's never been our home."

McSween walked over to the window and looked out at the tree-lined street. Blowing dust was kicked up by a summer rainstorm to the west.

"Susan, it is our home."

On July 15, the main body of the Peppin posse rode into town through the billowing dust of a windstorm. After occupying the Wortley, they fired a volley at the McSween home. Billy and his group left the Tunstall store and rushed into the McSween house through the back door. Some of the posse went through town to the building next to the courthouse.

"If they want a fight we'll give it to them," Billy declared as he watched from a side window as some of the posse lined up behind trees near to the hotel. "What kind of men are they? Shooting at a house with women and children. And at a man who doesn't even carry a gun."

For four days, the two groups exchanged rifle fire with little effect. Neither side knew what to do to end the stalemate. A cavalryman delivering a message was fired upon. His horse was killed. Who the shooter was or which side he was on was not known. This infuriated Colonel Dudley who received word at his office at Fort Stanton. On July 19, the Colonel marched into Lincoln with troops, a cannon, and a Gatling gun. He promptly informed everyone that, if his troops were fired upon, he would respond with cannon and the rapid-fire gun. The soldiers set up across the street from the courthouse on the west end of town. For whatever reason, the Colonel aimed his howitzer at the two small stores occupied by the McSween forces. The men in the buildings retreated out the back to the river, with some going to the McSween home. Although the big gun was never fired, its presence had been enough of a threat that, within several hours, the only building occupied by the Regulators was the McSween home. Inside the house, along with the men, were Susan and Elizabeth with her five children.

29

At 2:15 in the afternoon of that same day, Susan McSween declared she was going out to talk to Colonel Dudley. She opened the front door, one arm held high waving a white handkerchief. On the way to the Colonel, she passed close by a small house where the Sheriff was watching her through a window converted into a gun port.

"You coward," Susan yelled, "firing on women and children."

"Have the fugitives surrender and it's over," Sheriff Peppin responded.

"Woman and children are in that house, stop shooting."

"Get them out."

"To be shot?" Susan screamed.

"Have the men surrender. They're safe in my custody."

"Like Tunstall." She grabbed her full skirts and ran.

Colonel Dudley, striding out to the front of his men, met her in the middle of the street.

"Colonel, I implore you, stop the fighting." Susan stood directly in front of Dudley, her eyes blazing, looking directly into his.

"I cannot and will not interfere with law officers performing their legal duties."

"Women and children are in our home, the one you're shooting into."

"My men have not fired a shot."

"Others have."

"Not my men."

"Colonel, for God's sake stop the fighting. Women and children are in that house," Susan said loudly, her face only inches from Dudley's.

"Get them out."

"Women and children are going to be killed."

"Get them out. Don't you understand English? Get them out."

"So the men can be killed?"

"Get the women and children out. The men can give themselves up."

"My husband will be killed if he surrenders."

The Colonel did an abrupt about face, paced smartly away from Susan, and stood behind the cannon, refusing to even look toward her.

"You're murderers, all of you," she screamed. "Murderers! Murderers!"

A few of the men in blue looked down, but most looked away, up the street toward the house under siege.

Susan glared at the Colonel who still refused to look at her. She turned and walked back to her home. No shots were fired while she was in the open. Once inside, she could hear the bullets beginning to hit the adobe bricks.

"He will not stop the fighting," Susan said to her husband and the men standing beside him. Billy and O'Folliard had their rifles pointed out the barricaded windows.

"We will all be killed," her husband said.

"Get a gun," Billy said, turning to look at him.

"No, I will not shoot men."

Billy glanced at Susan for a moment before turning back to look for targets in the street. There were none.

By four o'clock, members of the posse had managed to start a fire around the wooden door frame of Susan's kitchen. The blaze engulfed the room and started the sofa blazing in the next room.

"Susan, you must leave," McSween said. "You and your sister with her children."

"I won't leave you."

"You must. While there's light I'll step out with a white flag."

"Alex, oh no, I can't."

"Get your sister, the children."

The two women and five children stood at the front door.

"Go next door to our store. They are no longer shooting at it. My men have deserted it."

Susan grabbed Alexander and clasped him to her. For a moment neither moved. Finally McSween stepped away.

"I will never see you alive again," Susan said, holding tightly onto her husband's hand.

"Then in the next world."

Her arm dropped to her side.

He cracked the door and shoved a white flag tied to a cane into the opening. "Women and children are coming out," he yelled before stepping out onto the porch. Two bullets thudded into the adobe bricks beside him. He stood without moving, staring toward the hotel. The gunshots ceased.

Elizabeth Shields, clutching her nine-month-old baby along with her memoir tablet, and with her other four children in tow, followed Susan McSween. They clustered together then rapidly walked to the store next door. When they were safely inside, there was only silence in Lincoln. No one from either side fired a gun for minutes. Then one shot echoed through the town, then another, and soon bullets were again thudding against the adobe house.

By seven o'clock, the fire had spread, beam by beam, room by room, through one wing and into the front of the McSween house.

"It's time to pray," McSween said to the men who had retreated to the sitting room next to the kitchen in the opposite wing, the only two rooms not ablaze.

"No," Billy said. "It's time to fight."

When O'Folliard tried to hand him a pistol, McSween pushed it aside. The young Texan looked at Billy who only shrugged.

The sound of rifle fire continued to echo from the buildings in town with muzzle flashes visible from one end of the street to the other. The men in blue were becoming dark forms, hardly visible against the dark trees along the river.

30

By nine o'clock, it was dark, but the blazing house lit up the area. The Regulators were all crowded into the kitchen except for McSween. He sat in the inside doorway on a small footstool with a Bible in his hand. Rifle fire was sporadic.

"Yea, though I walk through the valley of the shadow of death…," McSween, his head bowed, spoke in a firm voice clearly audible in the kitchen.

"We've got to make a break for it," Billy said to the men surrounding him.

"We'll be shot down like dogs."

"No," Billy said. "That adobe fence throws a shadow in the backyard. They won't see us till we run out the back gate. Make it to the trees at the river. They won't come looking."

"It's our only chance," someone agreed.

"The first ones that go will have the best chance," Billy said, "catch them by surprise."

"I shall fear no evil, for Thou art with me…,"

"They'll be waiting on the next bunch," Billy said. "And the last ones better run fast."

The men checked their Winchesters and pistols.

"Me and O'Folliard will go last," Billy said. He walked back to McSween, shook his shoulder and again offered him a pistol, which he refused.

"We've got to make a run for it." He grabbed the man's arm, pulling him to his feet, guiding him into the kitchen.

In single file all the men slid out the door and into the backyard, with Billy and O'Folliard at the tail end. They were shielded by the adobe wall. When the first men went through the gate and reached the open area, shots rang out, bullets whistled by. Those in front ran, but some in the middle turned and ducked back behind the wall. Billy and O'Folliard darted past them, sprinted through the gate and zigzagged rapidly toward the trees. In seconds the two had disappeared into the trees along the Rio Bonito.

The gunfire remained intense, hitting the top of the wall, the middle. The men left behind remained crouched down. Running through the gate was now certain death.

"I surrender, I surrender," McSween yelled over and over. The shooting stopped.

A deputy entered the back yard, pistol in hand.

McSween stepped toward him. "I will never surrender."

Gunfire immediately resumed. The deputy fell dead with a slug to his head.

Bullets slammed into McSween killing him. The two standing beside him crumpled, dead. Hijinio Salazar, hit twice, crawled to safety. The shooting stopped. The posse had no other targets. The flames of the fire raged, but only an occasional shot rang out.

At sunrise the house was smoking ruins with four dead bodies strewn in the backyard. The soldiers were sitting on the edge of the street in front of the court house, some leaning back against the trees asleep.

By noon a grave had been dug in the vacant lot beside the plot where Tunstall was buried. Lined with white cloth, an open pine coffin holding the body of McSween rested beside the grave. Susan bent over the casket, caressing the hand of her husband that held a Bible against his chest. The part-time undertaker had dressed the body in a black suit and vest, and white shirt with a dark tie. No gunshot wounds showed.

"You were never meant for fighting. I guess you've found your peace," Susan said her voice quivering. "Alexander, you were the best man of them all."

She stood up straight and motioned to the four men to place the rectangular top on the coffin. Susan stepped back but not before glancing into the box. Her eyes, with no tears, looked down on her husband's body for the last time. After nailing on the lid, they lowered the casket with ropes into the grave.

The Presbyterian minister, who had just performed the burial service, stood by Susan. She picked up a handful of sandy earth from the freshly dug pile and pitched it into the grave, hitting the coffin with hardly a sound. She turned and walked away saying nothing, her body unbending, her lips in a grim straight line.

In the Lincoln cemetery, three graves were being dug, two for the men who died with McSween and one for the fallen deputy. The Reverend walked down the street toward the new graves where the white pine coffins rested on the sandy ground. Across Lincoln an absolute silence set in. The Reverend bowed his head and began to pray.

31

On July 20, Colonel Dudley and his troops returned to Fort Stanton. They were followed by Peppin who had spoken with the Colonel about the fate of Brady. He had told the Colonel that he planned to remain at the fort for some time. With the Sheriff gone, the bodies of their men buried, and Tunstall and McSween dead, the posse disbanded. Dolan, concerned about his life in Lincoln, left for Santa Fe.

Earlier that same day, Billy and O'Folliard, linked up with Fred Waite, John Middleton, and several others, who had escaped from the Tunstall store. They all walked along the Rio Bonito to a small farmhouse a mile from Lincoln. They were fed, reluctantly, by the family living there who feared retaliation by the Dolan supporters. At several small ranches, Billy and his friends stole horses then rode into the hills.

There were over a dozen of the Regulators, Billy included, bent on remaining a force. In the following days, they raided the Mescalero Indian Reservation for horses. The Indians' agent assistant was killed while trying to prevent the theft. Afterwards Regulators ended up in Fort Sumner where they were welcome. After a small but fine baile, the Coe brothers called it quits with the Regulators and prepared to ride north.

"Billy, you ought to come go with us," one brother said. "Ain't nothing here for you. Just get yourself killed."

"No," Billy said his hand on his pistol, his thumb rubbing its hammer. "Things ain't been settled yet."

The Coes mounted and without looking back at their friends reined their horses around, heading north. Billy and the others silently stood in the street watching the two as they rode into the distance.

"Charley, how do you feel about staying and fighting?" Billy finally asked, turning to Bowdre and his neighbor, Scurlock.

"I'd like to get back to farming, to my wife," Charley said, "but I'm not going to quit."

"One thing," Billy said. "you ought to get away from your farm, only a dozen miles from Lincoln. That close they'll come looking for you."

"I hate to leave my farm, the cabin we built."

"I'll help you move, but we got to do it now."

Charley nodded.

"The other thing is Pete Maxwell is looking for hands," Billy said. "You two can be full-time cowboys. Settle down."

A month later, on a warm August evening, Billy and the Bowdres sat outside of the small one-room adobe house where Charley and Manuela had moved near Fort Sumner.

"It's mostly over for me," Charley said. "I've got a job, a house to live in." Turning to look at his wife, he smiled. "And there's other things on my mind."

"I want Charley at home," she said.

"Si, si, yo comprendo," Billy said.

"There's Doc Scurlock down the block playing with his kids," Charley said. "We want to do the same."

From Fort Sumner, Billy, Fred and the remaining men, excluding Bowdre and Scurlock, raided a number of small ranches whose owners had sided with Dolan. With a horse herd gathered, the group headed to West Texas and sold their stolen stock. They made friends with the Panhandle ranchers but, after three months, Billy was ready to head back to Lincoln.

"I'm heading back to the Indian Territory where my tribe the Chickasaws are living," Fred said. He, Billy, and O'Folliard, late one night, sat in a small bar in Tascosa, Billy with his coffee and the other two with beers.

"Fred, during all the fighting you were a good friend, my best. I hate to lose you."

"It would've been good to start our place on the Ruidoso, but it wouldn't work."

"No, not until things settle down. Somebody would take a potshot at us sooner or later," Billy said.

"You the best fighter I've ever seen, ever heard of. One on one, you could take any man around. But that's not for me. I don't really like shooting people."

Billy pushed the cup of cold coffee away. Tomorrow he would say goodbye to Middleton and Brown who were headed east, too, for someplace down in Texas. Billy liked New Mexico where all his friends were, where they had the good bailes. But there were lots of enemies there too. Across the table was one of his best friends, Fred, who was right to be getting out, going back to his people, no doubt about that.

The next morning Billy mounted up, watching as Fred and the other two headed toward the rising sun. O'Folliard sat on his horse next to Billy. Slowly, the three rode out of town never turning to wave goodbye.

Shortly Billy and his sidekick rode westward toward Fort Sumner.

Billy rode along through the creosote bushes saying nothing to O'Folliard trailing behind. It was the end of something, thoughts told her as much. She would miss Fred, his companionship, someone who had always stood by her side especially when the bullets were flying. The thing was that she had never had the urge to tell Fred her secret, as good a friend as he was. He was a friend, man-to-man. She would probably never see him again and that saddened her. Another thing, with those black, black eyes he reminded her of Pat Garrett. When things were sliding downhill, thoughts of the tall lanky man always seemed to intrude. When back in New Mexico Territory, she would like to see him and talk some about life. Was Billy ever going to be able to reveal the truth to Pat? The notion to do so was certainly in her head. But maybe in New Mexico that could never be done. She had followed a long trail and its ending was nothing but a blur, if that.

32

Billy, Tom O'Folliard, Doc Scurlock and Charley Bowdre sat on straight-backed cowhide bottom chairs around a rickety table. They were in a room of abandoned Fort Sumner, constructed from adobe brick. It was late November of 1878. The Kid and O'Folliard had ridden in from the Panhandle that afternoon around five o'clock. Scurlock and Bowdre were sipping whiskey from a quart bottle, while the other two ate biscuit and steak sandwiches Manuela had put together.

"Kid, things got changed," Charley said. "The President of the United States replaced Axtell as governor with Lew Wallace, a Civil War general."

Doc tilted the bottle for a big swig.

"The President," Charley continued watching Doc take another long drink, "put out a proclamation for the men of both sides to put their guns down and go home. Doc, you just got back from Lincoln with all the news. Why don't you give it to Billy?"

"Well, here it is. Wallace, the governor, put out a proclamation too," Doc said. He placed the quart bottle on the table and ran his hand through his hair while giving Billy a grin showing a big gap where his two front teeth had been knocked out in an earlier scrape. "I drank a hell of a lot of liquor in Lincoln, but I got all the words Wallace put out straight."

"Go on," Billy said.

"The Governor declared a general amnesty for everyone who was fighting in and around Lincoln."

"Except here's the kicker," Charley butted in. "It doesn't count if a man's already indicted. Like me for shooting Roberts on government land. Or you, Billy, for the Brady shooting and the fight there at Blazer's Mill."

"Guess me and Tom, we'll just hang around Sumner, see how things go," Billy said.

"Don't think you'll have trouble in Lincoln," Doc said. "Peppin lost the election in November and he's doing nothing. Laying low at Stanton. Probably thinking about Brady. George Kimball won. He's the new sheriff but can't do a thing till January when he's sworn in."

"And you two, what are your plans?" Billy asked.

"Stay in Sumner, work for Maxwell, go home to our wives at night," Charley said.

"Here's something. Susan McSween's back in Lincoln from Vegas," Doc said.

The last week in December Billy walked out of the Wortley hotel and mounted up. He rode slowly east out of Lincoln on the Roswell road into the flat grassland of the Pecos Valley. He had been talking to Susan and a man she had brought with her from Las Vegas. Huston Chapman. He was a loudmouth, someone Billy didn't care for. Susan said her plans were to bring charges against Colonel Dudley, one man of several she held responsible for her husband's death. Chapman, though unarmed, was causing problems by confronting Dolan, Jesse, and his men. He acted as though he wanted to get the shooting started again. Exactly what Billy did not want. All of that was in the past. The shooting, the killing. Maybe Susan was right—the Kid, as she now referred to Billy, and men like him were responsible for getting Mr. McSween involved and committed to the fighting. They should have given him the opportunity to use his knowledge of the law to get things settled in the courts. Billy kept his horse at a slow walk, turning north toward Sumner. Remembering Susan's words brought on a frown. But what was someone suppose to do when a friend was gunned down? Just let it go?

Billy reined up. Large dark clouds were moving in from the west, low like a snow storm was on the way, and Sumner was still five days away. Far to the east many small dark shapes were visible, Chisum's cattle grazing on the brown grass. One day Billy would ride down and visit with Old John, as Chisum was now called. See what his thoughts were and maybe settle an argument over whether or not the rancher owed Billy money for fighting for the Tunstall, McSween, Chisum side so they could keep their store and bank open. Billy prodded his horse forward.

One thing, it seemed like Doc and Charley were out of it if the fighting started again. With Manuela wanting her husband home and babies, Billy was pleased that Charlie seemed happy to have a steady job, that he didn't seem interested in rustling livestock. That was something his friend had started doing only after the killing of Tunstall and McSween. Where did that leave things? It left Billy with one good buddy, Tom. Working on the Coe ranch was no longer a possibility, the two brothers having gone north. Maybe he'd just go back to dealing Monte.

For him to stay around in Lincoln though or any place in the territory— there was something that had to be done. He needed to get amnesty, promised by the Governor, for him and Charley. From the word going around Lincoln, the new sheriff Kimball was serious with plans to arrest anyone with an outstanding warrant. If Susan's new friend Chapman got things stirred up so the shooting started again, Billy damn sure didn't want to be fighting the law and the Dolan bunch, both at the same time. Talking to the sheriff was something that was going to have to happen. After that, the Dolan gang could be faced.

33

By February of 1879 Billy was dealing Monte in the bar of the Wortley Hotel in Lincoln a few nights each week. He'd talked to Sheriff Kimball. It was agreed that until the governor's amnesty proclamation was fully understood by everyone, who it applied to and who it didn't, and if Billy caused no new trouble, he would not be arrested. At least not for now.

Early one evening Billy stood at the bar with a cup of coffee. Tom drank a beer with Hijinio Salazar, who had recovered from the wounds he'd received escaping from McSween's burning house.

"A year ago, they killed Tunstall," Billy said, staring down at his reflection in the dark wooden bar. Just above his head a coal oil lamp hung from a beam, casting a cone of light over the three men.

"You evened it out, getting Brady," Tom reminded him.

"Yeah, maybe."

"Billy if you want to do some more fighting, I'm with you," Tom said.

"Like I said, no I don't. That's why we all agreed to meet with Dolan, Jesse and that gang."

"You know, whatever you say we'll do," Tom said.

"Depends on them," Billy said. "I asked to get together and have everybody agree to stop the fighting. It's up to them."

Later the three men, with several others who had ridden as Regulators, were standing on the north side of the street in Lincoln. Dolan, Jesse, and eight of his gang stood on the opposite side. For several long minutes, no one from either side said a word. Their arms hung loosely, hands close to their sidearms and, as agreed, no one held a Winchester.

"Kid," Jesse said. "I don't think we can trust you one fucking inch."

Billy leaned back against a hitching rail, but his hand remained close to his holster. "I'm not here to start the bullets whistling. Don't want to."

"I trusted you once, let you ride away without a fight and look what happened."

"Jess, starting a peace parley with a shootout, that's not my plan."

"You killed two of my men, Morton and Baker." Jesse stepped to the front of the men on his side of the street.

"I'm here to make peace. We all done some shooting putting slugs in other men." Billy said.

"You saying we should just forget about the killings? My two men you gunned down?"

"Jess, you want a fight. Let's get the party started." Billy stood up straight, ready. "But me, I don't want one."

"I think Billy is right," Dolan said quietly, but clearly and emphatically. He stood next to Jesse. "He asked for this meeting. It makes no sense for us to keep on killing each other. There's nothing to be gained."

Jesse glanced at Dolan and slowly looked back at Billy. A silence settled in, except for the sound of a piano someone was playing in a bar down the street.

"What the hell," Jesse said. He walked to the middle of the street where he met Billy. "Let's call it even and go get a drink No more killing each other and no testifying in court."

He and Billy shook hands.

"Anyone breaks this agreement I'll kill," Jesse yelled.

For several hours the two groups mingled in the bars drinking heavily, all except Billy who finished only half a beer. Tom stayed close to Billy and drank nothing at all. Leaving one bar, the group walked down the street, heading for another. Campbell, one of Jesse's men, staggered along in front of the others.

Huston Chapman, unarmed as usual, walked down the middle of the street. He ran into the group coming face to face with Campbell. The two had words and Campbell drew his pistol, yelling for the other man to dance.

"I'll not move my foot one inch for a drunken mob."

Campbell jammed his pistol into Chapman's chest. Billy standing over to the side said nothing. Dolan drunkenly drew his pistol and shot into the air. Campbell's finger reflexively jerked, firing his pistol into the chest of Chapman who crumpled to the ground dead, his vest smoking from the point-blank shot. The group continued down the street totally ignoring the body.

Billy figured, that with the gunplay, Sheriff Kimball would be looking for him and slipped away. Shortly he and Tom rode out of town. Whether anything had been solved Billy didn't know.

34

Governor Lew Wallace and old Squire Wilson, the Justice of the Peace who had deputized the Regulators, sat in a darkened room in Wilson's small home in Lincoln. The light came from one candle on a wall shelf and the glow of the red coals in the fireplace. The two waited on their appointment with The Kid. The time and date agreed upon by Billy and the governor was nine in the evening on March 15, 1879. It was fourteen minutes after the hour and the two men continually glanced at the large gold pocket watch on the table and then at the door. Curtains had been drawn across the two windows.

Wallace had been in the town for five days. In that time he had replaced Colonel Dudley with an experienced captain. The new commander immediately arrested Campbell and Jesse, vowing to prosecute the men who had murdered Chapman in cold blood, as that had happened after his proclamation of immunity. The killing had been the final straw. The incident caused the governor to act, to finally visit Lincoln, something he had promised months earlier when he had been appointed to replace Axtell. After arriving, he had received a letter from Billy saying he had witnessed the slaying and would be willing to testify if the governor would give him a pardon for all of his past actions. Wallace, urgently needing a witness, asked for a meeting to discuss what could be done along those lines. He said that he was certainly amenable to doing something about amnesty for Billy or perhaps initiating a pardon.

"You think he'll come?" The governor looked at the watch again shifting in his chair and pulling on his goatee. "And alone?"

"He's always done what he's promised, both the good things and the bad. But on this, I just don't know."

A soft tapping on the door caused both men to look quickly in that direction. The door opened and Billy entered, a Winchester in his left hand and his 41 Colt in his right, both cocked. He stood there looking around, first at the two men then at a blanket covering a rectangular opening leading to another room. Finally he looked back at the two men. Their hands lay motionless on the table. With his heel, he pushed the door shut. He crossed the room where he jerked back the hanging blanket with his right hand and pistol, the barrel level. It was a small kitchen, dark, hardly lit by the candle light. Billy checked the two men, who had not moved, and again stared into the dark room before releasing the curtain. He moved to stand next to the fireplace. The entrance was now directly in front of him.

"I'm here to see the governor." Billy's two guns pointed at the floor.

Wallace slowly rose. His hands, with fingers spread and palms forward, were held in front of him chest high.

"I'm Governor Wallace."

Again Billy studied the room, especially the doorway covered by the blanket. After a moment his eyes returned to the standing man.

"I'm Billy Bonney."

"Glad to meet you," Wallace said, not moving, hands remaining half raised.

Billy let the hammer down carefully on the rifle, placing it against the wall without glancing away from the other two.

"We're the only ones in the house." Wallace lowered his hands.

"I figured. I've been watching the house for several hours. Sitting over there in the trees along the Bonito." Billy uncocked his pistol, sliding it into his holster in one smooth motion. Just as quickly, he removed his heavy coat, hanging it on a wooden stub stuck into the adobe brick. During all that movement, his eyes had remained fixed on the two men. The butt of his 41 pistol gleamed slightly in the dim candle light and, though holstered, the leather holding strap was not snapped over the hammer so a quick draw was clearly possible.

"I appreciate you coming as I asked," Wallace said as he glanced at Billy's pistol. "And alone."

"I keep my word."

Governor Wallace, now standing tall and ramrod straight like the general he once was, took a few slow but deliberate steps toward Billy, extending his hand which Billy shook.

"You care to have a seat?" Wallace indicated a chair against the wall, which faced the entrance that Billy had just walked through and gave Billy a view of the doorway with the blanket.

Billy sat down on the edge of the chair, his one arm resting on the table and the other on the arm of the chair, his hand hanging down almost touching his pistol handle. Tunstall was the last man who had shaken his hand without hesitating. And this man the governor, though larger and older with a wrinkled face and so unlike the Englishman, still reminded Billy of his friend. Someone who had given Billy a chance for a fresh start in life. Perhaps the Governor could be trusted.

"We've got things to talk about," Wallace said, seating himself directly across from Billy.

The two agreed. The Kid would testify and Governor Wallace would grant a pardon for all of Billy's past deeds. The governor pointed out that both Evans and Campbell were in jail in Fort Stanton. To protect Billy while he testified and afterwards, he would be arrested and jailed as though he too were going to trial. But in fact it would be a form of protective custody. And that was something he would need because of the deal Billy and Jesse had made that night in Lincoln. The Dolan bunch would certainly be after him for going back on his word, something he did not feel sorry about. Tunstall's death was still with him. Nothing had happened to change the way he felt about the killing of his friend.

"I'm putting my trust in you," Billy said.

"When this is over," the governor reassured him, "you will have your pardon and be a free man unwanted by the law."

The two stood and shook hands.

Billy slipped his coat on and grabbed his Winchester, quickly checking the chamber. He blew out the candle, leaving the room lit only by the burning log in the fireplace.

"You have my word on this," the governor said.

In the flickering light Billy stood without moving, almost eye to eye with the stern looking Wallace. His blue eyes bored into the brown ones. Suddenly The Kid gave his nonchalant smile and walked out the door.

35

The following day, March 16 1879, Billy was eating a late breakfast in the home of a Mexican family in San Patricio. Over the years, he had pushed a steer or two, unbranded, into their rickety corral. A man walked in to tell The Kid that both Jesse Evans and Campbell had escaped from the jail at Fort Stanton. After finishing his meal, Billy wrote a letter to Wallace promising to fulfill his part of the bargain but, he emphasized, when he was arrested as planned, the governor should make sure it was by men Wallace trusted.

Sheriff Kimball, with a small posse, arrested Billy and O'Folliard the next day. They were placed in a home next to the Montano store where Wallace was staying. The two were free to move about as they pleased without being harassed by the sheriff, who was well aware of how the easy arrest had been arranged.

On April 14, 1879, in the Lincoln County courthouse, Judge Bristol opened the proceedings for the murder of Chapman. Billy and Tom testified against Campbell, Evans, and Dolan, who was the only one of the three present. When the jury recessed to decide on a verdict, the two stood outside leaning against the hitching rail.

"We've done out part," Billy said. "I guess Governor Wallace will hear about it back in Santa Fe."

"He could have been here," Tom said.

"Don't matter if he keeps his word. The real question is, where's Campbell and Evans."

"There're probably in the middle of Texas by now, somewhere."

Billy looked square at his young friend. "Tom, you watch out, pay attention. Either one would shoot us if they got the chance. In the back maybe."

"If I don't shoot them first."

"You just take care." Billy's eyes never left Tom's until both turned to walk back into the courthouse.

The verdict was read by District Attorney Rynerson who was the prosecutor. Campbell and Dolan were indicted for the murder of Chapman, Evans as an accomplice. Dolan secured a change of venue and walked away. At Fort Stanton on May 12, Colonel Dudley was brought to trial for arson on the charges presented by Mrs. McSween. Billy testified as to the Colonel's involvement and substantiated all the charges, but the man was exonerated.

Weeks later, back in Mesilla, Judge Bristol and Rynerson charged the U.S. Marshal of the Territory, John Sherman, with bringing in William Bonney and Scurlock to be tried for the murder of Roberts on federal property. The marshal did not act immediately. Although the word got back to Lincoln, Billy remained free to walk the streets. But he was well aware that it was only a matter of time before he would be taken back to Mesilla to face Bristol and Rynerson. Both were Dolan men and determined to convict The Kid. Of this there was no doubt in Billy's mind. Clearly the governor had done nothing, and evidently he had gone back on his promise of a pardon. Also no one had heard of where Jesse might be, although there were rumors that he had disappeared into Oklahoma, the Indian Territory.

Late one evening, in the middle of June, Billy threw a few items into his saddlebags and headed his horse toward Las Vegas. But by the end of summer, he was back in Lincoln. Sheriff Kimball talked about arresting the Kid but took no action. Yet that threat was always present, so Billy rode north for Fort Sumner.

His friend Bowdre was still there working for another rancher who had bought Pete Maxwell's cattle. In the cool of the evening, Billy, Charley, and his wife sat outside by the side of their small adobe home close to Fort Sumner.

"Doc Scurlock and family left last week," Manuela said. "Gone back to Texas where he's got folks."

"From what I know about Texas, no one's going down there looking for him," Billy said. "So he's out of it."

"I'm glad for him, really glad. He's alive," Manuela said, glancing at Charley. "But I cried when they pulled out. All the children leaving. I loved every one of them as though they were mine."

"Honey, it's okay," her husband said, reaching over to cover her hand with his. "We're going to have some of our own, just a matter of time. Now that I'm home every night."

"I miss the children already," she said close to tears.

Billy glanced over toward the west when Manuela covered her face with her hands. The sun had disappeared behind Capitan Mountain. Charley put his arm around his wife. Billy stood and walked out to his horse, turned to say something but remained silent as the two held each other tightly. Neither looked toward Billy who mounted and walked his horse away.

Having children, it was a world that Billy knew nothing about. How it happened, sure that was clear. But why these two weren't having any or couldn't was a mystery. Clearly both wanted to have a baby. What did it take? A man and women going to bed once, a hundred times? Billy glanced over his shoulder at the two sitting close together. Darkness was closing in.

In Fort Sumner, the bars were packed most nights by the ranch hands from all the small spreads. The bailes were held weekly and were well attended. Billy went often, but sat out most of the dances.

Billy often ran into Celsa Gutierrez who was always with some good-looking Mexican man. She often gave Billy a smile, flashing her small white teeth, especially when she was dancing and caught his eye. Yet Billy never butted in while he tapped his foot and watched the others.

The truth when Billy faced it head on was that she was not in the mood to dance with women. Thoughts of Garrett often entered her mind, but Pat evidently stayed away from the dances. Billy didn't look him up, having heard that he'd married Apolinaria, his wife's sister.

Tom O'Folliard rode into town one day, saying there was a big market for beef over in White Oaks where gold had been discovered and the town was full of hungry miners. Also the Indian reservation needed beef since Tunstall's death and because Dolan was no longer in that business.

Billy, Tom, and some newly acquired friends, cowboys who had drifted north out of Texas, raided some of the small ranches and pushed the cattle into White Oaks. Sometimes they swung a wide loop and pulled in Chisum's cattle if his hands weren't around. They also raided the Texas Panhandle ranches for horses, selling them back in the territory. Occasionally Bowdre went along, saying the wages he was paid as a hand were not enough.

It seemed to Billy that the situation was right back where it had started, stealing livestock. The only difference was that now Billy was looked upon as the leader. He had counted on two men to give him a chance at starting a new and honest life, Tunstall and the governor. Tunstall was dead, killed, and the governor had failed to keep his word.

36

Christmas of 1879 came on a bright sunny but windy day. Billy and Tom spent the holiday with the Bowdres. The Kid had killed two wild turkeys while he was out riding, shooting the dried pods from yuccas with his Winchester. At the cabin they dunked the birds into a pot of hot water to loosen the feathers, plucking them under the direction of Manuela. She made cornbread dressing and giblet gravy as the two gobblers cooked. As usual a pot of pinto beans simmered on the stove and for dessert there was apple pie.

After the meal Billy and Tom rode over to their room in the crumbling Fort Sumner. They had fixed up two canvas pallets with blankets. No one in Sumner had heard anything from the governor or from any lawman. That no word came from Wallace bothered Billy. Testifying in court like the governor wanted had put his life in jeopardy if Jesse or any of his gang ever showed up again in the territory. And Billy was still under indictment, as was Charley, who was going straight most of the time. It was a hell of a note when a man wouldn't keep his word.

"Tom, Uvalde, you think it's a good town to live in?"

"Not for me. I been there, but yeah, it ain't a bad place."

"They got saloons, places to gamble, play Monte?" Billy slid his boots off, and slid under the canvas.

"Sure, the town's got that. What's on your mind?"

"Thinking things over is all."

"Maybe we'll go down there sometime. Introduce you to my kinfolk. Let you meet my grandma, the one who raised me. After that, you want to stay in town, good, but I got to see more of the country before I die."

Billy blew out the candle between them. Sumner was okay, but it wasn't too exciting even with the seven saloons. But a lot of friends were there. And it was convenient, situated on the west side of a growing cattle empire along the Pecos River. Since it was on the edge of the county, the sheriff from Las Vegas had no interest in visiting, which suited Billy fine.

Things had changed around town. Men had moved in from Texas and the Indian Territory. Garrett no longer worked as a bartender and was spending much of his time in Roswell. Billy remembered the tall, angular man well. How his black eyes always bored into anyone he looked at. Billy hadn't seen him since having that drink with him in Lincoln after his first wife died. The word was going around that after Pat married her sister he was doing better. Billy hoped so and wished him well. Yet thoughts of the tall man wouldn't go away.

On January 10, 1880, Billy with some of his Texas friends—most having been pushed out of that state by the Rangers—rounded up some Chisum cattle and worked over the brand, converting the long rail into a wavy arrow and slicing off the flap of the Jingle Bob ear cut. It was the way the brand was usually altered. They pushed the small herd into a narrow canyon and blocked the entrance with a line of cedar posts, haphazardly hung with barbed wire. It was their plan to herd the cattle into White Oaks after the brand healed and looked a little authentic. They would sell the cattle at twelve dollars a head to Pat Coghlan, who had a ranch on the west side of Sierra Blanca and dealt in stolen stock.

A week later Billy had a beer in a saloon in Sumner and got into an argument with a drunk. Billy left before there was any gunplay and rode out to check on the cattle. On the way he ran into Jim Chisum, John's brother. He was herding a small bunch of longhorns north. Chisum and his hands had discovered the cattle with the altered brands.

"Maybe some of the stolen cattle are mine," Billy said when Jim told him what he had found.

"You're welcome to look them over," Jim said. "We didn't see anything but cattle with the botched effort to change the long rail brand."

"Your word is good enough for me. No need to check," Billy said. "Why don't you leave your stock in the canyon and come into town. Have a drink on me."

After combining the two small herds, they rode into Sumner. It was late evening and the streets were muddy from the snow dumped on the small town a day earlier. Billy, Jim Chisum, and one of his hands dismounted and walked into Hargrove's Saloon.

"You men ain't from here," said a burly and obviously drunk man sitting at a table.

Billy smiled. "Grant, I met you this afternoon. You still in a bad mood, looks like."

"I'm looking for someone to kill. I ain't particular," Grant said.

Billy turned back to the bar, ordered a beer, and pitched a coin down when the other two ordered whiskey.

"You're John Chisum," Grant said, "and I been looking to put a bullet in you for some time. You always fucking with the little ranchers."

"Hold it," Billy said walking over to stand in front of Grant.

"I'll just shoot you first," Grant said.

Billy eased his pistol out of the holster, placing it on the table.

"Hell, you got a gun. It ain't like shooting an unarmed man. Pick it up," Grant said.

"Let's just trade pistols for a minute," Billy said, still smiling. "I'd like to see how that ivory-handled gun of yours feels, its heft."

Grant picked up Billy's gun and bounced it in his left palm several times. He pulled his own, pointing it at Billy before placing it in is his hand.

"Good feeling gun, good balance for a forty-five," Billy said, turning, aiming it at the window his back to Grant. Deftly he lowered the loading gate and spun the cylinder letting three cartridges slide out. Billy handed the single-action pistol back to Grant with the hammer on an empty cylinder and, at the same time, picked up his pistol from the table. Everyone was watching the two, no one talking.

"One thing, Grant, you got the wrong man, that ain't John Chisum."

"You're a lying little fuck."

"I got no fight with you," Billy said smiling and turned his back, walking away.

A small click sounded as Grant cocked the pistol, quickly followed by a louder clack when Grant pulled the trigger of the forty-five pointed at Billy's back.

The snap of the hammer hitting an empty cylinder was followed by two shots sounding like one as Billy spun, drew, and fired all in one motion. A red splotch appeared on Grant's lower lip and another larger one in the front of his throat as his head was knocked backwards. Grant collapsed onto the table tilting it, sliding off, crumpling to the floor, dead before he hit.

Billy looking through the gun smoke, gave his nonchalant smile to the half-dozen men staring at him. He rubbed his left hand across the smooth end of his pistol where the sight had been filed off for smooth drawing. After snapping the loading hatch open, he punched out the two brass casings and reloaded.

"It was a good game," Billy said holstering his pistol, "but Grant don't know how to play."

Chisum and his cowhand emptied their shot glasses and stood, motionless.

"You men ready for a refill?" Billy asked.

"No," Jim Chisum said. "We'll head back to the herd."

"Well, give me a mug of coffee," Billy said to the bartender. He sat down at a table, ignored the body on the floor but glanced at Chisum who looked straight ahead as he walked through the swinging door.

37

In the early spring of 1880, Billy, Bowdre and O'Folliard moved over a hundred head of cattle from the Texas Panhandle to White Oaks, once again selling most of the beef to Coghlan, and some to the meat-cutters in town. Stock detectives riding in from the Panhandle found hides with the Texas ranchers' brands hanging on the corral behind one of the butcher shops. But The Kid and friends were long gone, having ridden back to Sumner.

By October, Billy was tired of the bailes and dealing Monte for small stakes to the cowboys from little spreads. After all, dancing with women was not all that exciting to Billy. Taking a trip was appealing. What he was going to do was ride to Roswell and look up Garrett. See how the man with the black eyes was getting along. Billy had heard that Pat had finally moved to Roswell but without his new wife. He had been elected sheriff of Lincoln County on November 2, 1880, pushing for law and order. He was immediately appointed a deputy by Kimball, the current sheriff. Garrett was also appointed a deputy U.S. marshal. So Billy figured he ought to talk to Pat and find out what was going to develop between the two of them.

Pat and Billy sat in a small saloon in Roswell with the deputy drinking whiskey. Billy had his usual cup of coffee. It was late and, other than the bartender, the place was empty. Garrett was responding to a note from Billy asking to meet him there.

"You and your new wife doing okay?" Billy asked.

"We are, doing fine."

"I never see her around Sumner."

"She's there. Just don't get out much with a kid on the way."

"Heard you got elected sheriff last week."

Pat nodded.

"I was pulling for George Kimball," Billy said.

"Figures."

"We got along, I stayed out of Lincoln."

"Lincoln's not the problem."

"Guess me and you are going to be on opposite sides of the fence from this point on," Billy said.

"I got elected to clean this place up. Get rid of the cattle thieves one way or another."

"Dead or alive."

"That's the way it's going to work. Always has."

"Stealing livestock, it's something I was forced into." Billy looked at Pat's hands, lying easily on the table with his fingers relaxed. But his eyes were not. Those black piercing Indian eyes with the long eyelashes.

"Billy, why you rustle cattle don't matter. Not to me, not to no one. The ranchers around here name you as one of the major cattle thieves, as do the Texas stock detectives. That puts you at the top of my list."

"And the murder indictments? The ones Wallace promised to get dropped. Gave me his word."

"Whether he does that or not is between him and you."

Billy finished his coffee.

"As long as the indictments are there, I'm going after anyone that's got one." Pat tapped his pointing finger on the table softly three times, his mouth a hard straight line.

"Pat, I appreciate you being honest but, goddamn it, I ain't the only one who shot somebody. Nobody seems to give a shit about Tunstall being killed."

"The law is the law. Indictments are indictments. Kid, I can't change a thing."

"What chance do I have going to trial down in Mesilla, in court with Judge Bristol?"

"Like I said, I don't make the laws."

Billy pushed his chair back and stood. "Yeah."

"They are what they are and I'm going to enforce them."

"Figured you would."

"From one end of the county to the other."

"Figured that too."

"Kid, I'm the law now. But I'm doing nothing till I become sheriff unless I'm forced, even if I got on a deputy badge. So right now you're getting a free ride."

"You'll be a good lawman." Billy shoved his wide brimmed hat down hard on his head. "I heard about you getting the stolen horses back from the Comanches last winter. Just you and two others."

"Everyone else turned back when the food was gone. Me, I didn't. We tracked them for over a week. The thought of quitting never entered my mind."

"How many Indians were there?"

"Two kept going never stopped to fight."

"How many did you get?"

"Eight. I killed eight. The others got three."

Billy buttoned his coat, covering his pistol. He started to say something, but didn't. Instead he faced his friend, waiting on the black-eyed man to make some remark maybe about the two of them. But Pat said nothing.

Billy turned and walked out. There was no doubt about it, Pat was a tough hombre. Yet he was also the only man who might and could possibly make Billy disappear and a woman appear. Then the only thing necessary was to ride away, head for Texas, buy some clothes like the McSween woman. And Billy would be gone forever. Pat was the only man around who made her think about not being Billy, who made her whole body flush and feel warm.

38

Memoir, page 48

The Kid was doing enough to earn a name for himself such as his involvement in the killing at the Greathouse ranch. Except that wasn't the whole story. Newspapers started printing stories on the young outlaw. Some were true, others weren't. But the stories sold papers. After a trip along the Pecos River Valley, the editor of the Las Vegas Gazette wrote a letter to the governor complaining about the lawlessness of the entire region. The leader of the rustlers, the man responsible, was someone called Billy the Kid, the newspaperman declared. In December the paper published an article similar to the letter, also naming The Kid as the boss of the lawless gang. The story was picked up and printed by the New York Sun. Billy's notoriety was sweeping across the country.

Late on the evening of November 26, 1880, The Kid and a half-dozen outlaws sat around at the Greathouse ranch in the large kitchen, which also served as a bar. They had disposed of some rustled horses in White Oaks and had stolen merchandise from several stores in the small town. Dave Rudabaugh and Billy Wilson, two infamous killers, were in the group. Except for Billy, all were drinking liquor supplied by their host, "Whiskey Jim" Greathouse. The ranch was halfway between Las Vegas and White Oaks, a good stopping place.

The following morning, they awoke to find four inches of snow on the ground and the ranch surrounded by a posse sent from White Oaks. Asked to surrender, they adamantly refused.

Jimmy Carlyle, a member of the posse and a well-known blacksmith, volunteered to enter the ranch building if Greathouse would come out and stay with the deputized men until Carlyle safely rejoined the group. The men inside, drinking liquor again, searched the blacksmith for guns and found none. As the day wore on, Carlyle asked if he could return to the posse who now insisted they would kill "Whiskey Jim" if Carlyle was not released. The men in the house refused to let the blacksmith rejoin the posse.

The standoff continued until around two o'clock when someone outside fired a gun. The sound was loud and reverberated in the still mountain air.

"They've killed Greathouse," Billy Wilson shouted.

Carlyle immediately jumped through a glass window, tried to run and stumbled. The men inside started firing through the splintered window at Carlyle who pitched forward dead, shot numerous times. The firing ceased. Members of the posse backed away from the house, stunned at seeing their friend lying on the ground, his blood painting the snow red. Greathouse, unharmed, stood without moving.

"I ain't one of them. You fellows know me. I just sell liquor. " Greathouse said. He walked slowly back into the house.

Discouraged and cold, the posse fired a few shots into the adobe building before riding away to meet the wagon of provisions they had sent for. Discovering there was no one outside, Wilson and his men walked out the front door, mounted and rode back to Sumner.

Returning the next morning, the disheartened posse was not disappointed to find the ranch house empty. After loading Carlyle's body into a wagon, they set fire to all the buildings.

"One thing for sure, the people in town ain't never going to put out the welcome mat to Billy again," one of the men said. "Jimmy was liked by everyone."

They turned the wagon around and headed back to White Oaks, occasionally looking over their shoulders as the black smoke snaked upward in the still air. The wagon bounced along, its wheels following the two ruts.

In early December, 1880, Charley Bowdre, encouraged by Manuela, met secretly with Garrett who had promised there would be no arrest. Near dusk they met at a curve in a faint wagon road leading out of Sumner. Both men were armed but sat on their horses quietly, their hands crossed on the saddle horns.

"I'm quitting the gang," Charley said.

"When?"

"Soon as I can. Let Billy know I'm leaving. Moving to Texas."

"You need to do it quick."

"I know."

"Though Apolinaria moved to Roswell, she and Manuela remain good friends. Both want you to get out of here. Soon."

"I'm trying to get ready, buy a wagon."

"You still got that indictment, the Roberts killing, against you. While you're around here riding with Billy, from this point on, I'm going to be sleeping on your trail."

Charley nodded then jerked his wide brimmed hat down hard on his head.

"You get out of here because, you don't, I'll get you sooner or later," Pat said. "After you leave, I won't come looking for you. You got my word on that."

Charley looked Pat in the eye for several seconds, reined his horse around and rode slowly away, the darkness swallowing him. Soon rider and horse had disappeared. Pat shook his head. He put spurs to his horse and headed toward White Oaks. The Carlyle shooting on his mind.

In Santa Fe, the governor's assistant Baxter argued that the promise of a pardon was null and void. How could Governor Wallace grant clemency to a known killer and outlaw like The Kid? Too many illegal activities involving Billy had occurred after the promise. The papers would crucify Wallace if he were to let Bonney off.

"Along the Pecos Valley, the stockmen from Seven Rivers to Sumner are up in arms about Billy," Baxter said. "He's the boss of the rustlers and the ranchers know it."

"Well, I didn't guarantee any one action on behalf of The Kid," Wallace said to Baxter but mostly to himself. "I didn't."

"Governor, you need to, you must, do something to show your support for the law. Something that will gain the backing of the cattlemen."

On December 13, 1880, the Governor made the Kid infamous across the nation, doing the one thing that was required—the one thing that had been lacking. He put a price of five hundred dollars on his head and instructed Garrett to bring him in. Two days later a letter arrived from The Kid trying to explain and exonerate himself from all the accusations. Governor Wallace, a literary man now well known for authoring Ben-Hur, ignored Billy's note.

39

Sheriff Garrett and his posse had ridden hard to reach Sumner on December 19, 1880. A cold snow-storm was blowing in from the west off Sierra Blanca. In the little town, Pat had heard from friends that Billy and his gang were there. The posse carefully searched each of the crumbling adobe buildings. Nothing was discovered.

The men put their horses in a covered corral and entered the old hospital that still had a roof and was on the main road into Sumner. With the wind continuing to blow and the snow becoming heavier, they settled in for the night after starting a small fire in the rock fireplace. One posse member was posted as a guard.

"I guess this is as good a place to spend this kind of night as anywhere," a deputy said. It was ten o'clock.

Pat looked at him. "Billy is going to wind up in Sumner at some point in time. We just got to be here when that happens."

"He sure ain't going to be out traveling on a night like this."

The guard stuck his head in the door, "I hear horses coming."

"This kind of night, it's got to be Billy and his gang. Nobody else would be out," Pat said.

The waiting men grabbed their Winchesters and stepped out onto the porch under the overhang. Pat and one deputy leaned against the wall on the side of the building the horses were riding toward.

Billy and Tom rode along at the front of the column of six men with Bowdre bringing up the rear. The wind was gusting and biting cold. All had their hats pulled down over their foreheads and heads ducked low. They had ridden in from the Wilcox-Brazil ranch where they had packed away some butchered beef given to them not out of friendship but out of fear. They were heading into Sumner after being told by a sheepherder that Garrett and his posse had ridden away.

"We'll get into town, stay tonight. Get us some provisions tomorrow, head for Mexico," Billy said.

Tom said nothing, his coat collar whipping in the wind.

"Jesus, I need a shot of whiskey," Billy said and wheeled his horse around to ride to the back end of the column, figuring that Bowdre would have a drink.

O'Folliard rode up to the hospital building. His horse stuck its head under the overhang almost hitting the barrel of Garrett's cocked Winchester.

"Hold it," Garrett yelled.

Tom went for his forty-five. Garrett and the deputy fired, the slugs slamming into O'Folliard just under the heart. His horse started bucking in circles.

The other riders yanked the reins so their horses spun around to run away from Sumner. Each rode hard in a different direction through the creosote and mesquite bushes, soon disappearing in the snow and darkness.

"Get off that horse. Put your hands up," Garrett hollered.

Tom, his horse under control, rode slowly toward the building.

"Hands up," the Sheriff repeated, his cocked Winchester pointing at O'Folliard.

"Don't shoot, I'm killed," Tom said doubled over, his mount no longer moving.

Pat slowly approached the horse, his rifle still cocked. He slid Tom off his horse and carried him into the building.

Pat stoked up the fire and kneeled down to examine the wound.

"Must I die?" Tom asked, lying curled up on the floor.

"Take it like a man," a deputy said, looking down.

"Tom, you don't have much time," Pat said softly.

"Tell Grandma, I..." His eyes closed and his trembling stopped.

"He rode with a killer and that's what he got," a deputy said.

Pat glanced up for a moment then back at Tom. "Go check his saddle bags. See if there is anything there. Something that might let us know where they hang out."

Pat rolled Tom on his back and straightened out his legs.

"Only thing," the deputy said back in the room. "There's a letter to a Mrs. Mary Jane Cook, Uvalde, Texas. Says Dear Grandma."

"Well damn it," Pat interrupted and grabbed the letter. "We'll bury him in the morning." He rose from his kneeling position, walked over to the fire, and stood there. "I'll mail the letter," he said. "Put a note in it. She needs to know."

The gusting wind, the rattling sleet and the popping of the burning juniper were the only sounds. No one said anything. Garrett remained motionless, hands on hips, staring into the flickering blaze.

40

On December 22, The Kid, Bowdre, Wilson, Rudabaugh and two others were all asleep on the floor of a rock house next to Stinking Springs. It was three miles east of the Wilcox-Brazil ranch where earlier they had eaten. But thinking that Garrett and his posse might show up, they had ridden away. It had taken them almost three days to get back together after the ambush in Sumner.

Garrett and his men did ride into the ranch after the gang had fled. With a full moon and snow on the ground, it was not difficult to follow their tracks. Pat knew there was only one place the trail could lead. The rock house. There was no other shelter for fifty miles. At 3:00 in the morning, the posse reached Stinking Springs and, walking quietly, approached the building. Three horses were tied outside and snoring could be heard from inside.

Pat gathered his men. "That's them. Dawn gets here, they'll come out. The Kid is a hell of a good shot. We ain't taking no chances. When I recognize him, I plan to shoot. All of you start firing after I do."

With his men in good strategic positions in front of the house, Pat placed his Winchester on a rock, pointing straight at the door. He leaned back against a ponderosa pine and waited. When daylight came, a man stumbled out of the building, empting a grain bag in front of one of the horses. He straightened up and stretched. His arms raked the wide sombrero atop his head.

"That's Billy," Pat whispered and fired.

Immediately a dozen other shots echoed in the narrow ravine.

The man was slammed against the wall of the house, his hat falling. Someone reached out the door and grabbed the wounded man, tugging him into the building.

"Damn that was Bowdre not Billy," Pat said.

"You're killed," Billy said to Charley in the rock house. "Go shoot the sonofabitches before you die." He shoved Bowdre's pistol into his hand.

The wounded man staggered out the door and up the small rise, his pistol pointing downward. No shots were fired. He collapsed in the arms of Garrett who placed him on some blankets, dead.

Billy and friends were trapped. That afternoon a wagon of food that Garrett had sent for arrived from the Wilcox-Brazil ranch. The posse started a fire away from the rock house and placed the food in skillets. The scent of meat cooking was too much for the hungry men in the house. A white flag appeared in the doorway and the four men filed out, hands held high.

In Sumner, the prisoners were put in irons and fed. Afterwards Pat and Billy stood on the front porch of the Maxwell house.

"I hate to do it, but it's got to be done," Pat said.

Billy nodded.

"Got to go tell Manuela and leave her husband's body."

"It's my fault. I'll go with you, tell her first," Billy said. "I ought to have talked Charley out of going with us on that last ride."

Pat stared at Billy as both stood beside the wagon with the covered body.

"Get these chains off me. You got my word, no running."

For a while Pat didn't move, not even his eyes that bored into Billy. Finally he released the irons and swung up on the wagon. Pat kept the horse walking as they headed for Manuela and Charley's house.

Billy walked along quietly close to a turning wheel. "Pat."

"Yeah?"

"Charley liked to dress in a nice coat. When he had the money."

"I'd noticed."

"Right now they don't have a cent. Didn't have enough money to buy a wagon, get out of town."

Pat glanced down at the walking man who had stopped and was looking at him. He pulled up the reins.

"He needs a suit to get buried in," Billy said.

"Yeah, he does. You tell Manuela to buy one. Bill it against me."

"I appreciate that."

Pat snapped the reins to get the horse moving. After a block, he stopped in front of an adobe building, hopping to the ground.

Manuela stepped out of the door, saw the wagon and started running toward it screaming. When she looked over the side rails and saw the body, she continued to scream, ran and attacked Pat. Billy grabbed her arms and pulled her away, but she broke loose. She picked up a piece of split wood and swung it at Pat, hitting the forearm he held in front of his face. Billy locked his arms around her, holding her, pulling her backward. She continued to scream at Pat.

"It was me, not Pat," Billy said. "I got Charley killed."

Her screams died turning into loud sobbing.

Pat stood without moving, his hat off, arms dangling from slumped shoulders.

"It's my fault," Billy said. "All my fault."

She pressed her knuckles into her mouth, her eyes, crying.

Billy slowly, gently, walked her toward the house. The two stopped on the porch his arms still around her while she grasped for breath.

"Oh Charles, oh Charles," she wailed so low it was hardly audible.

Pat hadn't moved.

"No babies, no babies ever. Oh Charles."

Billy walked her through the door into the small back room. Manuela crumpled face down on the bed, sobbing.

41

Memoir, page 52

The Kid was kept in the Santa Fe jail for three months, during which time he wrote the Governor over four letters, receiving no response. On March 28 he was placed on a train and taken to Mesilla to stand trial for both the Roberts shooting and the killing of Sheriff Brady.

Judge Bristol convened federal court on March 30, 1881, to try Billy for killing Roberts on government land. His defense attorney argued that at the time the land was not under the jurisdiction of the U.S. government. The judge dismissed the case, but ordered Billy to stand trial in the Territorial Court for the killing of Brady. It was the same court and same judge.

Albert J. Fountain was the defense attorney. Billy was found guilty and, on April 13, 1881, Judge Bristol ordered Billy returned to Lincoln. On May 13 he was to be hung. The next day a reporter asked Billy if he thought Governor Wallace would grant him a pardon. Billy said he didn't think Wallace would, but he should because Billy was the only one of the many combatants who was destined to suffer the extreme penalty of the law.

On April 21, 1881, Billy was taken to Lincoln, turned over to Garrett, and placed in a makeshift jail on the second floor of the old

Murphy-Dolan store. An iron clasp was riveted to his right leg and a chain anchored it to the wall. His left leg had a clasp locked around it with a chain that connected to his right one. His hands were cuffed together with a one-foot chain. He was guarded by the deputies Bob Olinger and James Bell.

"You're a no good cur. I ought to shoot you now," Olinger said, standing outside the room serving as a jail. Grinning, he pointed his sawed-off shotgun through the doorway, aiming it at Billy. "This Greener is loaded with buckshot, cut you in half."

"Go fuck yourself."

"Don't mess with me, I'd soon do it as not."

Billy closed his eyes and laid his head back against the wall.

"I got four more hours till Bell takes over." He cocked both hammers. "All I got to do is say you tried to escape."

"Give me a gun, let's do it. One on one."

"Like hell I will."

"Then shut your mouth."

"Pat said you make one move to get out of here, for me to fire away." He brought the gun up to his shoulder and aimed it at Billy. "Bang! Bang! You're a dead sonofabitch. Got what you deserve."

"Olinger, shoot or put the gun down."

The deputy uncocked the hammers. "I'll let it go for now. But I'm going do it first chance I get."

That evening Bell relieved Olinger and set a plate of food in front of Billy.

"Here's a spoon," Bell said. "Sorry I can't take the irons off your wrists. You just got to do the best you can. They cut the meat up over at the restaurant."

"Jim, that's fine. I didn't expect to be let loose."

"That Olinger sure hates you."

"He'd never meet me on the street, face to face."

"No he wouldn't, but don't you give him no excuse to use that shotgun."

Billy smiled and started scooping up the pieces of steak with the spoon.

42

Four days later, on April 24, Billy stood in front of a bucket of water. It was almost midnight. She glanced through the bars that had been riveted into a rectangular metal door. Billy slid the cuffs over her hands, removed the shirt and one leg of the trousers. It was her first chance to wash since arriving in Lincoln. Bell had brought the full bucket and a rag before he went off guard duty. From below she could hear Olinger snoring.

Billy looked down at her breasts as she ran the wet rag over the small humps. For some reason in the last year they had started to develop slightly. She smiled, wondering what the men would think after they had hung her and discovered she was a woman.

"Where the hell is Billy?"

She looked up. Garrett was on the stairs, only his upper body showing. He stared at her.

"For god sakes. What the hell?" Garrett bounded up to the second floor and stood without moving in front of the bars.

"Good lord almighty. For god sakes. You're a girl."

She faced him, saying nothing.

"What in the hell?" He sat down in the desk chair but kept his eyes on her. He shook his head, stood up and placed his hands around the bars.

"For gods sake, what in the hell?"

"You can call me Wilma."

"Wilma?"

"That's my name, always has been."

"Wilma. For gods sake, you're a girl."

She continued facing him.

"Wilma?" He leaned his shoulder against the bars but never looked away.

"You're the only one knows. I expect you to keep my secret."

"Billy, a girl."

She wrapped a blanket around her waist and sat down on the cot. "Well, you've seen everything."

Pat walked across the room and sat down on a desk, pushing papers to the side.

He removed his hat, shook his head, and ran his fingers through his hair. He pulled a bottle of whiskey from a drawer and drank a big shot. He looked at her and held up the quart, offering a drink.

She smiled at Pat and shook her head. There was nothing else to say.

He sat there, glancing at her then back at the bottle.

"You might as well come in and share my cot so we can talk," she said. A warm flush was spreading throughout her body.

Pat rolled a cigarette and lit it, blowing smoke at the floor.

"I guess you would have found out when you hung me."

"I ain't hanging no woman." Pat took another long drink. He placed the bottle on his desk, jammed his hat on his head, stomped on the cigarette butt, and walked out, never glancing at her.

43

A little before twelve the following night, Pat leaned on his desk, took a drink from the bottle then faced the woman in the jail cell. He had been in the room for fifteen minutes, saying almost nothing.

"Well?" she said.

"I don't know what to think," he finally said.

"Open the door and sit down. We can talk. I'm not going to try anything."

He placed the bottle on the desk and removed his gun belt before he walked over. Unlocking and opening the door of bars, he stood there.

"Wilma, call me Wilma."

His black eyes never looking away, he sat down beside her.

"Pat, you have the damnedest eyes."

"What the hell?"

"I am a woman."

"I saw."

She placed her hand on his thigh, hard and muscular.

He said nothing.

Wilma smiled and with her free hand took his and placed it on her thigh. His fingers lay there motionless at first, but gradually began to grip her leg firmly. She turned her face directly toward his, her mouth open slightly.

Pat touched his lips to hers but quickly stopped.

"I am a woman," Wilma repeated. Pat's fingers were warm even through the denim.

"What the hell?" Pat just shook his head.

She leaned against him and pressed her lips to his again.

He moved away.

She leaned further into him. She pressed her lips against his dry warm ones.

"My god!" Pat said, but his body was beginning to relax.

"It's been a long time," she said softly moving her hand slightly on his thigh.

Pat shook his head.

"I am a woman," she said.

Pat stared at her. "I know. I know."

"I've not been with a man, for years." Her hand remained on his thigh.

"It's been a while for me too," Pat said. "My wife pregnant and all."

She put both arms around him and kissed him, her lips pressing hard against his. He remained passive for a moment. Then abruptly he returned the kiss, his arms enveloping her. He sat up, turned and unlocked the clasp on her left leg. Between the two of them, they managed to get the chain on her right leg over the end of the cot and her Levis off one leg. He dropped his boots on the floor and stripped his trousers away. They were joined, pushing hard, with a rapid rhythm.

"Oh Oh….Oh Oh Oh, ……… Oh my god." She shuddered.

Pat moaned and stopped all movement. But he continued to hold her tightly, his body warm against hers. Then gently, his hands against the mattress, he pushed upwards, away, his eyes looking directly into hers.

Dressed in shirt and trousers, Pat sat beside Wilma, the blanket over her shoulders.

She said quietly, "Patrick, this was different."

He nodded, seeming to understand.

For a while she sat without moving, saying nothing else, leaning against him.

"I sure as hell ain't going to hang no woman," he said.

Wilma placed her head against his shoulder, covered his hand with hers, squeezing his fingers. Those long strong brown fingers that had intrigued her from the very first time they had met. She said nothing else. What was there to say? It was better than anything she had imagined over the years, when she couldn't stop thinking about Pat and how it would be to go to bed with him. The intensity had been almost more than she could stand. For the first time in her life she felt like crying.

"I sure as hell ain't going to hang no woman," he again emphasized, placing his arm around her shoulders.

She touched her fingers to his moustache, wide and black but with specks of gray.

He slid one boot on. "I'm going to White Oaks in a week."

"So we still have a few nights to spend together?"

"Yeah, I'll take the night guard again. And I've been thinking about things all day. I got something to say"

"Go on."

"I'm leaving a pistol in the outhouse beneath the seat, on a nail. You get it while I'm gone."

He pulled on the other boot.

"One thing, Bell is my friend, a good man. I don't want him hurt. Olinger, you can do whatever."

"You don't have to do that."

"I said I ain't hanging a woman."

"I want you to keep my secret."

"Wilma, I wouldn't know how not to."

Again she placed her hand over his.

"You get loose, meet me in Sumner. I'm going to think about some things. How we end the chase for Billy. Talk to Pete Maxwell."

She watched his face, the deep-set eyes.

"And you got to remember I love my wife. You get away, live as Wilma someplace. I won't see you again after Sumner."

44

On April 28, while Pat was in White Oaks, Olinger was eating lunch at the Wortley Hotel next to the Dolan store. Bell was watching Billy whose wrists and legs were still chained.

"I got to go to the outhouse," Billy said.

"Wait till Olinger gets back then we'll take you."

"Damn it, Bell, I got to go now."

"You can wait. I ain't taking any chains loose."

"I need to do it right now. Look, leave the chains on. Just take the one loose from the wall."

Bell stood up and removed his gun belt but held his pistol in his right hand as he watched the captive. Billy moved to the end of the cot stretching the chain as far as it would go to give Bell room to work.

"Kid, you try anything, you know I got to shoot you."

"Just unlock the chain on the wall. How the hell could I do anything with my legs and hands in irons?"

Bell opened the steel bar door and stepped in. He slowly walked to the opposite end of the cot from where Billy stood. He stuck the key in the lock and twisted. The lock snapped open. Keeping the pistol pointed at Billy, he pulled the chain loose from the steel ring. Bell backed out of the cell.

Billy gathered up all the dragging chains, wobbled out the door and down the stairs, almost stumbling several times. In the outhouse he turned around.

"Leave the door open," Bell said.

"How the hell am I going to escape from this fucking outhouse? Through that hole?" Billy jerked the door shut, dropped his trousers and sat down beside the round hole. Reaching through it, he felt a pistol hanging on a nail far to one side. Grabbing it, he stood. After pulling up his Levis, he shoved the short forty-five into the waistband. leaving his shirt hanging out.

"Hurry up," Bell said.

Billy stepped out and walked, wobbling, toward the front door of the store. Halfway up the stairs he slid the cuff from his right hand, dropped his leg chains, and pulled the gun.

"Hold it." Billy spun and faced Bell.

The deputy froze.

"Don't move. I don't want to shoot you," Billy said.

"How the hell?" Bell's eyes showed a lot of white. His arms dangled motionlessly.

"I'm backing up the stairs. You follow, several steps behind."

Bell spun, bounding down the stairs.

"Stop." Billy fired one shot high, three feet over Bell's head.

Bell hit the landing and continued down the stairs to the first floor where he stumbled to his hands and knees.

Billy took aim at the center of the back of his head but, before pulling the trigger, raised the sight and fired another shot above the crawling man.

Bell reached the door, opened it and bounded out.

Billy grabbed his leg chains and hopped up to the second floor. There he picked up Olinger's shotgun and stood at the window.

Olinger, hearing the first shot, ran out of the hotel into the street. Seeing a man stumbling and running out the door, he pulled his pistol. Blinking in the bright sunlight, he fired two shots into the man. Bell collapsed.

"Hey Bob." Billy pointed the Greener down, both hammers cocked.

Olinger looked up to see Billy with his shotgun. Billy pulled both triggers. The two loads of buckshot slammed into Olinger, knocking him to the ground. He didn't move.

For minutes there was no sound after the double blast. Several men on the street stood motionless.

"Hey, you go get the blacksmith." Billy recognized one of the men as someone he'd played Monte with. "You," he yelled at the other one, "go get my horse."

Billy grabbed a key unlocking the shackle from his left leg, but his right still had the riveted clasp with the two chains dragging along. He scooped up the chains, walked down the stairs and out the front door with the forty-five stuck in his belt.

Smiling nervously, the blacksmith, a Mexican man, worked on Billy.

"Pedro, I ain't going to shoot you, so be careful, don't hit my ankle with that chisel. Or I might."

Finally loose from the chains, Billy removed Olinger's gun belt and strapped it on. A dozen men stood on the sidewalk watching Billy in the middle of the street. No one said a word or made a suspicious move. Billy smiled and mounted. He rode west out of town toward San Patricio. It was good to be free.

45

Billy rode into White Oaks after dark and stopped at a small house on a side street. It was early May, three days before the date he had been sentenced to hang. Dismounting, he looked around carefully. Seeing no one, he walked to the front door. Several times he glanced in all directions before knocking. A light from a lamp shone through a small window.

The door swung open several inches.

"Hi," Billy said.

Susan McSween didn't speak for a moment.

"It's okay. No one is around," Billy said.

She opened the door and closed it immediately after he entered.

"Well, Billy, I certainly didn't expect you."

"I'm leaving the country. I wanted to stop by and say goodbye."

"I'm glad you did and sorry you have to leave. Sorry they prosecuted you. Letting all the others get off."

"Susan, you made me see things different from the first time we met."

"We had our talks. We did that."

"From that earliest meeting I thought a lot about what you said. From that time on, I tried to do what was right."

She stood close to Billy, her hand resting on his arm.

"There was just too much killing, shooting. I couldn't stop. I had been doing it too long."

"I know you tried. What we wanted just didn't happen. Didn't turn out our way."

"That's all in the past," Billy said.

"Billy, why don't you have a seat?"

He sat down on the end of the sofa when Susan sat down in the middle. Her eyes watched his face.

"I've remarried."

"Hope that goes right for you," Billy said. "I've heard other things about you."

"Oh?"

"Someone said you were going to buy a large ranch with cattle west of town here."

"Yes," she said, "I am. My sister, Elizabeth and her family will live with me. She is going to finish writing a memoir about what happened in Lincoln. "

"Hope that works out for you."

"Things will go right for me because I've got the money to buy a good ranch."

"Money?"

"Yes. I'll sell my cattle—not stolen ones either—to Fort Stanton and the Indian reservation. With the others out of the business, I'll have it all to myself."

Billy was silent.

She smiled. "About the money. Mr. McSween had the foresight to do certain things. He opened a bank account for me in St. Louis. With my name, it couldn't be checked by the lawyers in the court cases."

"I wondered."

"The account had ten thousand dollars in it."

"You deserve every penny." Billy stood. "I got to be going."

Billy blew out the lamp, held Susan for a moment and slipped out the door. Grabbing the saddle horn, he mounted up. Susan did deserve every penny, her husband killed, her house burned. The Fritz estate money went to the right person.

46

It was Wednesday, a quarter past midnight on July 14, 1881. Pat Garrett, having heard a rumor that Billy was around, squatted beside Pete Maxwell's bed in the dark room.

"So you haven't seen The Kid around?" Pat asked Pete who was sitting up, leaning against the headboard.

"Not here."

Angled moonlight from a two-foot square window in the west wall provided the only light. A dark form like a shadow moved through the bedroom's eastside doorway that opened in from the wooden wrap-around porch.

"Pete, those two men outside. Who are they?" the dark form asked.

There was no answer.

"Who's that beside your bed?" the same voice asked.

Still no answer.

"Patrick? Goddamn it, is that you?"

Pat Garrett's gun roared twice.

The form at the door slumped backwards, hit the wall, and collapsed face down.

"Who'd you shoot?" Pete yelled. "Pat, who'd you shoot?

"The Kid. I'd know that voice anyplace." Pat stood, his gun aimed at the still form.

Pete lit a candle and Pat kneeled.

No one spoke.

Finally Garrett said, "He ain't breathing. Let's get him outside on the porch."

Pat grabbed Billy under the arms while Pete took his feet.

"He sure as hell don't weigh much," Pete said.

"Yeah," Pat said.

"He's got lots of friends here," Pat said. "We need to get him in a casket, buried by sunup tomorrow before folks get out."

Pat blew the candle out as they lugged the body toward the door.

"Put him in the cemetery where those young soldiers from Fort Stanton are buried," Pat said.

47

A month later, Governor Wallace wrote Pete Maxwell saying he'd heard rumors that Billy was still alive. The Governor explained he was worried that if not dead, Billy might hunt him down for not living up to his misinterpreted promise on the pardon. In the note was a request that Mr. Maxwell dig up the grave, examine the body, and make sure it was Billy.

Pete complied and sent the Governor a letter.

It read:

Governor Wallace,

We dug up the grave. No doubt it was Billy, same hair, same build, same clothes. Billy is dead. It was certainly the body of a twenty-one year old Anglo male.

Your obedient servant,

Pete Maxwell

Epilogue

Around eleven o'clock on the night of August 17, 1895, Wanda Brooks walked out of the Acme Saloon in El Paso where she had been dealing Monte. Wanda, in a long dress that fit her slender, wiry body tightly, had long dark hair with a few strands of gray. Wearing a shoulder holster covered by a large woolen coat, she linked arms with John Selman, Jr., an El Paso policeman. Together they went to his room in the Sheldon Hotel. They were lovers and had been for several years.

The following day Selman arrested a drunken whore by the name of Beulah. She had been staggering down the street in front of the Acme Saloon. Struggling with her, he bruised both of her arms and accidentally gave her a black eye before he was able to toss her in jail.

On August 19, John Wesley Hardin, Beulah's boyfriend, went her bail of ten dollars. He cussed out Selman, saying if he saw him again he'd kill him. Hardin and the woman left together, walking slowly to the house where she worked. Later John Wesley went alone to the Acme Saloon where he played dice with a man named Hank. He rolled high numbers.

"Hank," Hardin said, "I tell you one thing. I see that Selman again, I'll kill the sonofabitch. He's a bastard. I mean to do it."

Hank laid a five-dollar bill on the bar and shook the dice in the round cup before rolling them out onto the bar.

"Everbody in here listen. I'm going to kill the Selman bastard," John Wesley yelled. He picked up the bill, looked at Hank and said, "You lose."

At a table in the back, dealing Monte, Wanda Brooks watched Hardin and listened to his raving as the dice continued to roll. The game went on for several hours that evening with both men drinking heavily. Hardin was facing the back door when John Selman Sr., a constable, walked in the front.

"Look out!" Hank shouted and ducked.

Hardin's pistol appeared in his hand as he spun around to face the entrance.

The forty-one slug caught Hardin behind his left ear, slamming through his brain and exiting beside his right eye.

Selman fired three times as Hardin was going down, hitting the already dead man twice, once in the shoulder and once in his arm.

Constable Selman was given credit for all three hits although, to some, hearing that the man had been shot from the front, it seemed as though the bullet that went through Hardin's head created a strange wound. The large ragged facial hole looked to be an exit wound. The bloody hole in the back of the head was small like an entry point.

Selman, wanting the notoriety of killing the infamous gunfighter John Wesley Hardin, went to trial and confessed. Pleading self-defense he was acquitted by a jury. The woman dealing Monte, Wanda Brooks, was never questioned.

About Frank Carden

As a youth, Frank F. Carden spent time on a three-windmill ranch and in the oil fields of west Texas. He's picked cotton and housed tobacco in Kentucky, worked on a shrimper in the Gulf, and served three years overseas in the Navy's Submarine Service. He received his PhD from Oklahoma State University and taught at New Mexico State University.

Carden's short stories have appeared in *Serape: An Anthology of New Mexico Authors, Writers Without Borders, Kaleidoscope, The Rambler*, and his story "Quarter Moon" was a winning selection for the 2004 Southwest Writers Contest. *The Prostitutes of Post Office Street* is his first novel.

Also by Frank Carden

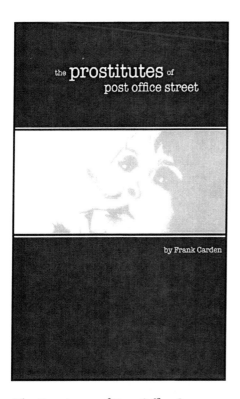

The Prostitutes of Post Office Street

Post Office Street drops readers into the red-light district of Galveston, where crooked cops and down-on-their-luck prostitutes dwell. Yet, in this seedy part of town, Carden paints a picture of hope as his characters seek to rise above the pain of broken hearts and misplaced passions.

CPSIA information can be obtained
at www.ICGtesting.com
Printed in the USA
FSOW01n0504221217
42676FS

9 781938 237188